ঠK

GW00771473

C0000 00180 0741

CHATEAU OF THE NYMPH

When Jenna goes to work in her aunt's French hotel, she finds that someone is determined to force her family out. Is it the darkly forbidding Luc de Villiers? Centuries ago, the son of the lord of the chateau had fallen in love with the girl from the village inn. Was history repeating itself? Only when Jenna's life is put in danger does she discover the truth behind the chateau's legend and find love in place of long-ago tragedy.

SHEILA DAGLISH

◆

CHATEAU OF THE NYMPH

Complete and Unabridged

LINFORD
Leicester

First published in Great Britain in 2009

First Linford Edition
published 2010

British Library CIP Data

Daglish, Sheila.
  Chateau of the nymph. - -
(Linford romance library)
1. Hotels- -France- -Employees- -Fiction.
2. France- -Social conditions- -Fiction.
3. Romantic suspense novels.
4. Large type books.
I. Title II. Series
823.9'2–dc22

ISBN 978–1–44480–374–7

Published by
F. A. Thorpe (Publishing)
Anstey, Leicestershire

Set by Words & Graphics Ltd.
Anstey, Leicestershire
Printed and bound in Great Britain by
T. J. International Ltd., Padstow, Cornwall

This book is printed on acid-free paper

1

The child asked her, 'Qu'est ce que vous faites?' Jenna was concentrating on the antics of an insect colony, disturbed when she'd lifted a large flat stone. 'What am I doing? I'm watching Albert.'

'Who is Albert?' The child crouched beside her. His English was fluent, although his accent proclaimed him French. 'I can see only ants.'

'That's Albert, trying to tug a dried grass leaf from his cousin.' She pointed. 'This little fellow — Oswald.' Smiling, she glanced at the boy. He was about six years old, she guessed, but his pristine white shirt and grey shorts weren't the usual tourist garb, and she knew most of the village children. He had come along the little-used track from the ancient fortress, above her.

Jenna had arrived from the opposite

direction, climbing the steps from the long street. Breathless, she had paused at the junction where two ways met. Normally, she would have turned to the right, towards the fountain, yellow-green in its coat of lichen. But today she decided to go to the left, hoping for a little peaceful solitude beneath the sombre stone walls of the ancient chateau.

From the terrace above the village, she could look down on mellow roof-tops and the wide road where small shops and cafés earned a living from the holiday industry. Beyond, the river was making its lazy journey towards Bordeaux and the open sea. Here and there, other steps and alleyways snaked upwards to where this higher line of honey-coloured buildings clung to the rockface. In places, tumbled walls were all that remained, but in their neglected vegetable patches gnarled fruit trees would soon be covered with blossom.

The boy was on his knees, studying the ants.

'Why do you move stones and watch the insects? I think that you are quite old for such a game.'

'Thanks a lot!' Laughing, she replaced the slab and said goodbye to plans for an uninterrupted hour's work, anticipating his next question.

'I like to draw tiny creatures like this. They're so busy and so funny that it's quite easy to dream up fresh adventures for Albert and his family.'

'You are a famous writer, then?' he asked, dubiously, assessing her jeans and white sweatshirt.

'I wish!' Laughter showed Jenna's white teeth against the light tan she'd acquired since leaving England four weeks ago. 'My parents hoped I'd become a teacher, but you need stacks of patience for that. What I really love is to write and illustrate children's books. The trouble is, they don't bring a regular salary!'

Critically the boy inspected her, from the copper tints in her straight fair hair, to silver-grey eyes, and down to well-worn trainers. Her chin was firm, a hint that she could be stubborn, despite the humorous tilt to her mouth.

Solemnly she inspected him in return. Olive-skinned, his hair was dark, cut short, presumably to quash any curls. The barber hadn't been able to subdue an endearingly snub nose. As the child's eyes met Jenna's, he grinned.

'You do not look like a teacher or a writer. My teachers are quite old,' he confided. 'But when summer ends I hope to be in Mademoiselle Jospin's class — she wears cheeky boots.'

He leant against the low parapet as, together, they scanned the distant river. The air was scented with wild herbs and grasses. Jenna drew in a deep breath. How she loved this place! Then she remembered why she was here. Surely it was madness to suspect there was a serpent at work in this Eden!

'So you are en vacances in France all summer?'

'No. I've come to . . . '

From higher ground, heavy footsteps

heralded the arrival of a man. The sun was behind him, casting his face into shadow, but outlining broad shoulders and blue-black hair. He seemed to be descending like some avenging angel, or, Jenna felt, with inexplicable apprehension, Lucifer himself. As he came closer, she realised he was aged about thirty and attractive, except for the frown which made his black brows a straight and forbidding line. Beneath them, cold green eyes caused her to straighten her shoulders and mentally prepare for battle.

'Mademoiselle, you trespass!'

Since he spoke in English, Jenna guessed that he had overheard at least some of her conversation with the boy. Flushing as she noticed the direction of his gaze, she nudged Albert's stone back into position.

It made no difference. He looked ready to explode but something told her that, unlike a volcano's heat, his eruption would shower thousands of ice-splinters. Even so, his attack made her step backwards.

'You will find nothing here. There is nothing to interest you and your kind!'

'I didn't know I was trespassing! And even if I am, there's no harm in picking up a stone or two!'

'You are wrong! It is wise to leave the stones of this estate untouched!'

'It's only a lump of footpath, for goodness' sake — which I've replaced.'

He blocked the way, as if he were expecting Jenna to charge past him. For an instant, she was tempted to do just that, just to see his reaction. Her lips quirked. Noticing, his mouth thinned even more.

'Today the path, tomorrow a piece of wall. And then you will search for an open window, to look inside. That is how your mind works!' The boy touched the stranger's arm. Presumably this was his father. Poor lad!

'Mademoiselle means no harm. We have been watching the ants.' Pink with embarrassment, he glanced apologetically at Jenna.

'And soon mademoiselle will discover that your home is the chateau and will use your long friendship for an invitation to enter.' His eyes met the boy's in an unspoken message.

Jenna watched this byplay, forgetting her annoyance, until her aggressor, hands planted on hips, tilted his head meaningfully at the downhill path. His rudeness made her blink.

The child bit his lip, then bravely defended her.

'Mademoiselle is not a newspaper reporter. She writes stories and draws pictures for children.'

'Then she should know that one does not make speedy friendships with small boys,' came the suave reply. Returning his cold gaze to Jenna, the man's lips scarcely moved. 'You take advantage of our bad fortune. Like others, you will resurrect the old legend and manufacture a great new story.'

'I've no idea what you're talking about!' Jenna had begun to suspect their identity. But she was thoroughly rattled by now. Usually even-tempered by nature, when pushed too far she could explode like fireworks. The tremor in her midriff came from anger, not fear.

'Come, Guy.' The man turned the boy towards the uphill track.

Her anger instantly fled. Guy was the young heir who recently lost both father and grandfather. Oh, heavens, what had she said? Impulsively, she put out a hand to stop them.

'I'm sorry! I realise now who you are. And of course I've heard of your terrible loss. I would never intentionally intrude. And I'm not a journalist.' A black eyebrow rose as she stumbled disjointedly. 'As for the legend, I can barely even remember it now.'

Guy prompted her. 'Chateau de la Nymphe was not always named so.'

'Of course!' Long ago, the lord's standard would have fluttered above the great rounded tower and, beneath it, a cluster of homesteads. As medieval kings and princes battled for supremacy, there would be time — time for glances to be exchanged, attraction to turn to love, and love to end in loss.

A harsh voice dragged her back across the centuries.

'Your memory lapse is quite realistic.' He didn't believe her. 'I suggest you consult a history book. In the meantime, I will trace your editor and complain that you harass children and should be moved to another department.' His lip curled. 'Classified advertisements, perhaps?' How could such a deep and attractive accent sound so unpleasant?

Dislike shaded Jenna's eyes to silver. The contrast they made with her pale golden skin and shining hair was striking but she didn't notice the expression of awareness in his face.

'I've had enough of you!' She'd done her best but he really was an offensive pig. 'I met your father and your brother once. I liked them. They were gentlemen.' A flicker in his eyes noted that she didn't place him in this category. Grabbing her sketchpad and pens, she turned to go. 'I've no interest in you or your wretched legend!'

Gently, she touched the child's downcast face. 'I enjoyed meeting you, Guy.' For his uncle's sake she added a deliberately final, 'Goodbye.'

She felt two pairs of eyes, one hard green, one dejected brown, watch her go. As her ankle turned, she slowed. There was no sense in breaking her neck, especially if 'Lucifer' could still see her.

A bubble of humour surfaced: he'd love to see her carried off on a stretcher. What a monster! Good luck to his wife — any woman who'd fallen for him would have her work cut out. She'd soon give up trying to tame him, content to be an exquisitely dressed aristocratic doormat. Chuckling, Jenna hitched her bag high up on her shoulder.

At the foot of the gradient, she walked towards the Auberge des Fleurs. But then, crossing the road, she went to the riverbank. Sitting, she stared at the glistening waters without really seeing them. Almost reluctantly, she looked over one shoulder, to where the chateau hung, starkly outlined, on the rocky escarpment. Was Guy being scolded? She hoped not. He'd been a lonely little boy, looking for companionship.

His uncle had obviously warned him — not only of strangers, but of newspaper reporters in particular. Jenna frowned as she tossed a pebble into the water. What was he trying to hide?

2

Aunt Elspeth was busy in the kitchen when Jenna returned to the auberge. The building was the smaller of two hotels in St Justin. Tucked beneath a vertical wedge of rock, it had been an inn for as long as anyone could remember. Even before the main holiday season, a constant trickle of visitors stayed for a night or two, drawn by its breathtaking location.

'Did you find some nice beetles?' Her aunt's busy fingers were rolling pastry cases, before tucking them into baking tins.

On the central workspace, Arnaud, their chef, was filleting fish with the aid of a ferocious knife and a warbled aria from *Carmen*.

'In the name of the saints!' Pausing, he glared as a clatter came from the dining room, empty of customers at this

12

hour. 'Soon there will be nothing left!'

Suzette, their waitress, was the daughter of a local widow, Madame Boulet. Elspeth had soon realised why Madame Boulet didn't employ the girl in her own small souvenir shop.

Something had shattered. Another plate? Again, Arnaud's aria came to a halt. They exchanged glances. No one spoke.

The restaurant adjoined the kitchen. It seated fifty diners, and afforded panoramic views of river and country-side. Near the door stood a massive dresser. Ornamental dishes decorated the upper shelves but the elaborate base unit was crammed with bottles, crockery and glassware for the dining area. Beside it, a curtained alcove hid a clutter of cleaning materials and bar stock.

'I'll clear it out next week.' Elspeth's regular promise was a standing joke.

'Did I find any nice beetles?' Belatedly, Jenna answered her aunt's question. 'Mmm. I came across an ant with a promising personality.' Perched on the workbench, in the familiar comfort of the kitchen, her confrontation with the stranger began to fade.

When Elspeth arrived here as a bride ten years ago, she had made kitchen renovation a priority. Arnaud's appointment later guaranteed the hotel's reputation for excellent food. She had shown no serious interest in men until, in her early forties, she fell in love with Philippe Brisset, astounding her family by her speedy marriage. Jenna had often holidayed here, whilst Elspeth and her husband built up the business, inherited from his father.

'Is there news from the hospital?' Jenna knew that Elspeth would have telephoned Philippe. It was six weeks since his accident and initially her aunt had been forced to close for a few days. They had been worrying about a spate of cancelled bookings, but his absence made the lack of clients almost welcome.

'Philippe sounded cheerful enough,

but I know his shoulder and spine are painful. It's the need for heart tests that frustrates him most.' With a nervous jerk which spoke volumes, Elspeth slid a loaded baking tray inside the oven. 'I'm just thankful that his accident brought the problem to light.'

She pushed back greying curls, her eyes resting warmly on her niece. 'He sends his love and thanks you most sincerely for coming to our rescue.'

'No problem. Fate organised it for us! Uncle P gets flattened by a rock, and I get a chance to talk to Albert.' As Elspeth raised an enquiring eyebrow, Jenna laughed. 'My little ant, of course!'

Rinsing flour from her hands, her aunt sighed. 'I still can't believe Philippe's accident happened. There are a few places where rocks might work loose, after torrential rain. But not above this building.'

Jenna nodded. The cliff behind the Auberge des Fleurs appeared solid. And yet boulders had crashed onto the patio where Philippe often worked on his accounts. 'But the rock just crumbled?'

'Crumble is too small a word.' Arnaud stood, knife raised, his white uniform topped by the red kerchief around his thick neck. Completely bald, his black eyes were sunk so deeply into his fleshy face that when he laughed, which was often, they almost disappeared. He reminded Jenna of a gingerbread man — although she'd never tell him.

'I know you dislike the truth of this, Madame, and the gendarmerie stays silent but you can be sure they will be watching. There are always young vandals whose brains are made of petit pois.'

Lifting the jug from the hob, Jenna filled three coffee mugs and took a jug of cream from the refrigerator. 'How many reservations have we this evening?'

'The two couples who stayed last night, plus a family of four checked in.' Elspeth sipped her drink with a murmur of pleasure. 'The Hargreaves won't be here to eat.' The brothers, geologists, had stayed here last year and found it a convenient research base.

'So there's only eight?' Jenna replaced a lettuce in the vegetable rack.

'The Selwyns will be back for dinner. So that makes ten.'

Mr. and Mrs. Selwyn, an English couple in their fifties, had also stayed the previous year. They spent their time searching for old books for their antiquarian store in London, which specialised in publications from Europe.

'Let's hope we pick up more bookings before evening.' Jenna started pulling leaves from an assortment of salad-stuff.

'Spoken like a true hotelier!' teased Elspeth.

'Remember I'm only here because your lovely husband isn't. The heat and holiday hordes might get to me by August. I'll tell visitors to chuck their money in the door and buzz off home!'

Arnaud's big and beefy hand deftly swept fish scraps into a stewpot. 'We hope that you, also, do not buzz off!

17

Not for many weeks!' he said cheerfully.

Jenna's arrival had enabled Elspeth to concentrate on the paperwork normally done by Philippe. The unanswered telephone had also lost vital hotel and restaurant bookings. With their savings ploughed into improvements, the couple now had little financial leeway.

Suzette, a wafer-thin girl with short black hair, poked an unsmiling face around the door.

'I will return this evening!' she announced, and was instantly gone.

'We await her return with impatience,' growled Arnaud, as he winked at Jenna. 'She is eager to meet her new beau.'

'I didn't know she had a boyfriend.' Jenna was surprised.

'She let it slip,' said Elspeth, 'But shut up like a clam again when I asked if he was a local lad.'

She glanced at Jenna. 'How far did you walk today?'

'Mostly upwards.'

'To chateau or fountain?'

'Chateau. Perhaps it's enchanted — or at any rate, I met the Beast!' She made a face. 'He accused me of trespassing. But the small boy with him seemed friendly enough.'

'You must mean Luc de Villiers and Guy, Hugo's only son. I'd heard they are here for a few weeks. Luc must be having a difficult time since his father and brother died in that dreadful sailing accident.'

'Yes, Mum showed me your letter.' Jenna's mother was several years older than Elspeth and avoided computers, insisting that handwritten 'snail mail' had more personality. Jenna enjoyed living in her own small flat, in a Devon market town, but frequently spent time with her parents, thirty miles away. Being an only child, she could well imagine Guy's desolation at losing a beloved parent. 'I'm so sorry for the little boy.'

'It's very sad,' agreed Elspeth. 'Guy inherited a nightmare that Luc must sort out. It's no secret that the old Count struggled to keep the estate. Hugo had to leave and earn a living with computers, and Luc is an architect.' Opening the oven, she tested her pastry. 'The chateau will become a dilapidated holiday home for the family, empty for most of the year.'

'Perhaps they'll sell it?'

Elspeth shook her head. 'They'd need to be desperate. The de Villiers family built it centuries ago. Isn't that so, Arnaud?'

The chef flung herbs into his simmering stock.

'Indeed, that is so, Madame. Marcel de Villiers, the first Count's son, accompanied Richard Coeur de Lion to the Crusades and fought beside him for lands in France.'

'Goodness, that's really going back some!' Jenna recalled the autocratic jaw, the confident stance of Luc de Villiers and began to understand. Lord of all he surveyed — except that his nephew was the real heir, she interposed, slightly maliciously. No wonder he'd tried to chuck her off the estate. But why accuse her of snooping? She put her thoughts into words.

'The sudden death of the Count and his eldest son was much reported in the Press,' said Arnaud. 'There were many reporters here, asking questions about the family and the old legend.'

'And that was . . . ?'

'In the early days, Marcel fell in love with the innkeeper's daughter, a beautiful girl. Even so, he still went to fight alongside Richard.'

'Some people in England regard Richard I as a king who was never at home,' said Jenna. 'It must be because we love the Robin Hood legend.'

'I believe he did hunt in Sherwood Forest once,' said Elspeth. 'When he was dealing with his unpleasant brother, John. But, of course, Richard was French, and very possessive of his French heritage. He often fought in this area — it is said he could be brutal to his enemies. Not so lovely at all!'

'But he must have had charisma,' mused Jenna, 'Or Marcel might not have abandoned his lady-love in order to follow him.'

'Legend has it that the girl gave birth whilst Marcel was away, but the baby died. Then she was falsely told that he would marry a high-born lady from the court of Eleanor of Aquitaine.' Elspeth's voice dropped, as though ghostly shadows were listening. From the window, a great bend farther upstream showed how the river had carved its way through the centuries. 'She threw herself into the waters there . . . and drowned.'

'Was this building the inn where she lived?'

'Almost certainly. Look at the thick stone walls and flagstone floor. It was probably built at the same time as the chateau.'

'You said the girl was falsely told that Marcel was to be married,' said Jenna. 'So it wasn't it true, then?'

'No. When he returned and found

that she and the baby were dead, he was beside himself with grief. When his father died, Marcel renamed his fortress Chateau de la Nymphe and set up a marble statue of a nymph — supposedly the image of his lover — in the courtyard. He never married, so the estate eventually passed to a cousin.'

'How dreadfully sad!'

'If it is true!' Chuckling, Arnaud waved a wooden spatula at Jenna. 'Save your tears, ma petite! Keep them for the onions.'

A thunderous crash came from the restaurant. They all went rushing to the door, where they stood, aghast.

The heavy shelves had fallen from the old dresser. Smashed on the floor, a mass of crockery and glass was being lapped by a seeping flood of wine.

Amongst the wreckage sprawled the body of a man.

Through bloodless lips, Elspeth whispered 'It's Mr. Selwyn!'

Mr. Selwyn had begun to stir as they reached him. He was a tall man and, although slightly stooped, was heavily built.

'Help me get up.'

Arnaud bent to feel his limbs. All seemed well, so he helped the older man to a chair. Ashen-faced, he was shaking from head to foot. Splinters of crockery and glass frosted his jacket. His shirt was stained with wine from the bottles lying shattered across the floor. Breathing heavily, he leant back, eyes closed.

Elspeth ran to telephone the doctor, but collided with Mrs. Selwyn.

'Robert! What . . . ?' In an instant she was bending over her husband. 'Someone! Get an ambulance!'

'Stop!' Mr. Selwyn pulled himself upright. 'Nothing's broken! Look!' Gingerly, he moved his arms and legs, and turned his head from side to side.

His wife's horrified eyes went to his shirt front.

He laughed weakly. 'For goodness' sake, Rachel, it's wine. Not blood!'

Despite his attempts to minimise

what had happened, they knew the weight of the dresser could have killed him. At last Mrs. Selwyn calmed, but insisted on driving him to hospital. She turned on a visibly shaking Elspeth.

'You should have foreseen this accident, Madame Brisset! The furniture here is too old and unsafe!'

When they left, Arnaud examined the fallen shelving. The long oak chest which formed a separate base was untouched. Although the smaller unit had rested, seemingly firmly, on this base, for some reason the entire upper structure had overbalanced.

'The problem may be that Suzette placed too much weight there. Then it toppled — pouff!' With a flourish he clapped his hands together. Seeing Elspeth's white face, he patted her shoulder in a clumsy gesture of sympathy. 'We will clear the mess, Madame. Later you can make the decision to repair or destroy.'

Briskly, he seized one wooden end and glared at Bertrand, the cellarman, who had appeared and was standing, mouth agape. 'Lift!' bellowed Arnaud. 'I cannot do it alone!'

The outside storeroom was dark, crowded with boxes and haphazard stacks of garden tools. The men heaved the unit into the central space where thick slabs covered a disused well.

The following morning, the Selwyns appeared for breakfast as usual. Rachel Selwyn was composed, but distant. Normally she had a ready smile but today the lines of her face were taut and even her hair was severely drawn back into a carved wooden slide. Still attractive in middle-age, her casual jacket and slightly flared skirt were in warm terracotta and flattered her generous curves.

Fortunately, the hospital check-up had been reassuring but, although she made no secret of her wish to return home, her husband had obviously persuaded her to stay.

'Yesterday's little contretemps was actually my wife's fault,' he said, winking at Jenna. She appreciated his desire to return things to normal. 'I'd crept into the restaurant to order champagne for dinner — her birthday surprise.'

'I can do without surprises in future!' Rachel Selwyn's voice was acid.

'Well, I hope we can make up for it tonight,' said Jenna, mentally putting another celebration bottle on ice. She knew that her aunt had offered to refund the cost of the couple's accommodation in compensation for the accident — a loss which the business could ill afford.

The incident had badly upset Elspeth. Later, she told Jenna that she and Philippe might sell the business, although they hated the thought.

'We've already had so much bad luck this year. And we've recently received two good offers. An attorney in Paris keeps pressing us to sell. And Auguste Jalabert is keen to buy.'

'Is that the man who owns the Coq d'Or?' Jenna had never been inside the larger hotel in St. Justin, but had met its owner.

Elspeth nodded. 'We're getting older and less able to cope with problems. Philippe's health must come before everything!'

This afternoon, Jenna welcomed the chance to climb high above St Justin but, for once, she failed to appreciate the scenery or the scented air. Her thoughts were chaotic. First, the cancelled bookings. Next, Philippe could have been killed — and was badly injured — by an inexplicable rockfall, and now one of their guests had been harmed. Whatever Arnaud's opinion, surely the dresser shelves were too stable for an overload of bottles to topple them? Could someone . . . ? No. What a crazy thought! Irritably she swatted a fly from her arm. But the fear persisted. Could someone have hidden in the alcove, waiting, then given the dresser a massive shove? Impossible!

It would be unfair to share her suspicions with Elspeth; her aunt was already worried sick. But, if someone was playing practical jokes then they were dangerous ones and could kill. What if they were not jokes? Jenna shuddered.

What was that? She listened. The call came again. Just below her were the remains of the ancient bakery in a tangle of ivy and bracken.

'Hello?' she called out.

A small voice answered her. Whoever it belonged to, they were in trouble. Scrambling over the wall, Jenna reached a tunnel of brambles. At the far end was a cleft in the rocks.

'Guy!' Ignoring thorns that tore at her skin and clothes, she inched her way towards the child.

'Mademoiselle!' His smile wobbled as tears trickled down his cheeks. 'My foot is held fast.' He had dislodged several small boulders which were now trapping his ankle.

'Don't worry! I'll soon get you out. Keep still.'

A valiant chuckle came from Guy. 'I can do little else!'

29

Jenna smiled. He'd got courage, this little boy. But what was Luc de Villiers doing, letting him roam into danger? And where was Guy's mother?

One by one, she lifted the rocks.

'Can you stand?' As she gently felt his ankle, he winced. With a sinking heart she realised he wouldn't be able to put any weight on it.

'I'll get help.'

'No, no! Please do not leave me!' He couldn't control his tears.

'Don't worry! I won't go,' she promised, with an inward sigh. 'We'll manage somehow.' She had nothing to support his foot with. He'd feel every jarring step as they struggled home.

By the time they reached the chateau, they were both exhausted.

'I am so thirsty I think I shall drink a whole bucket of water!' Guy's face was scarlet, as was Jenna's.

As she pushed open the gates, Luc de Villiers strode out to meet them. Jenna took one look at his expression and braced herself.

'What have you done to the boy? I warned you to stay away!'

'Uncle Luc, mademoiselle rescued me. I fell and hurt my foot!' Guy's uncle snatched him from her hold.

But suddenly Luc de Villiers noticed Jenna's appearance. She was angrily aware that she looked a sight. His hard eyes moved across the muddy streaks and torn threads on her once-white jeans and blue sweatshirt. They glinted green mockery at the silky tangle of hair which was clinging to her hot cheeks. His eyebrows lifted and a muscle twitched beside his mouth.

Jenna had no difficulty reading his thoughts: 'Hail the original scarecrow!' she muttered. Grinding her teeth, she started heading for the downhill path.

'Not so fast, if you please! This time I will have your name.' He paused. 'And the name of your newspaper. 'Refuse Collectors' Monthly', I assume?'

Jenna was in no mood to share the joke. Gravel scattered as she spun to face him. 'I've told you . . . I'm not interested in your family, or your rotten castle! All I care about is your nephew — which is more than I can say of you!'

If scowls could kill, then she was a dead woman but a small sound of distress from his side silenced him.

'Guy, I apologise.' The harshness left his voice as he held his nephew closer. 'You understand why I must . . . ' He was interrupted.

An elderly woman in a black dress and voluminous white apron hurried from inside the building.

'Mon pauvre petit!' Talking non-stop, she began to usher Guy, still in his uncle's arms, towards the open door. But then she noticed the girl who had begun to walk away. 'C'est Jenna, n'est pas?'

Reluctantly, Jenna turned. Her hand was clasped and vigorously shaken.

'Hello, Madame Dupont. It's good to see you.' There would be no quick escape. Jenna had known the French-woman since those early holidays in St Justin, when the housekeeper would often visit friends in the village.

The woman's sharp eyes rounded. 'What have you done to yourself?' She shot a comprehensive glance at Guy. 'Has this naughty boy been in mischief?'

Luc de Villiers intervened. 'A slight mishap only,' he said, frowning, 'You know this . . . lady?' Hastily, he substituted the word for whatever he'd really meant to use.

With her usual honesty, Jenna inwardly admitted that he was justified. His casual shirt and well-cut trousers revealed quiet good taste, worlds apart from the grubby mess that was Jenna Edwards!

Madame Dupont was examining Guy's scratched legs. 'I have known Jenna since she was a little girl. She came to the village when Philippe Brisset from the Auberge des Fleurs married an English lady, her aunt.'

'Jenna,' his deep voice repeated slowly, and Jenna, with an unexpected lurch in her stomach, felt as though she had never before heard it spoken.

'How is your poor uncle?' Madame Dupont didn't wait for a reply. 'As for your aunt — how glad she must be that you help her!' Without pausing for breath, she gave her opinion of vandals who caused accidents, the morals of the younger generation, and the approaching nuptials of her youngest grandson.

Jenna was swept into the chateau and even Luc de Villiers was helpless before the flow. When they reached an immense, timber-ceiling kitchen, the housekeeper went to fetch ointment and plasters whilst he inspected Guy's swollen ankle. 'I think it is a sprain, but we will have an X-ray, to make certain.'

Jenna cleared her throat. 'Now that Guy's safe, I'll leave you,' she said, edging towards the door.

'Nonsense!' came the bland reply. 'We have established that you are an old friend. You cannot hurry away!' He rose swiftly to bar Jenna's exit, then took drinking glasses from a cupboard, completely at home in the kitchen. Stone walled, with a huge cooking range, it was well used, judging from the orange lilies on the long refectory table, and the wonderful aroma of warm bread.

'You are taking time from your city occupation to be Good Samaritan in St Justin? When must you return to work?' Her identity might have been established but she felt that he still didn't trust her. Why was he was so concerned about his privacy?

Madame Dupont had returned. 'Jenna is an artist and a writer par excellence! One day she will be famous!'

Her outrageous flattery and Jenna's grimace brought an unexpected grin to Luc de Villiers' features. Suddenly aware that he was the most attractive man she'd ever met, she took a deep drink from her glass. Tragedy, depriving him of father and brother, had left him to safeguard his nephew's shaky inheritance. Luc looked as though he didn't smile enough. It was hardly surprising.

'I should have consulted Madame Dupont before today,' he murmured, a gleam in his eyes. 'One has no need for local newspapers.'

Jenna's answering smile lit her features to the fragile beauty of Botticelli's fantasies. The man watching her became strangely still.

When she left, Luc de Villiers walked with her towards the gate. Although his manner had eased slightly, was he making sure she was off the premises?

A statue occupied the centre of the pebbled yard. Weather-stained, the once-white marble figure faced across the battlements, to where the river soon became lost between folds of hill and crag.

'Oh, this is lovely!' Jenna breathed, gazing upwards. The slender nymph stood poised to fly.

Delicately carved, she was a girl at the dawn of womanhood. Lifted to the skies, her face yearned for something — or could it be someone? — far beyond her reach. 'Is she the reason this place is named Chateau de la Nymphe?'

Luc de Villiers looked from the statue to Jenna's intent face and spoke softly, almost to himself. 'There is an uncanny resemblance . . . ' Then, his lips resumed their customary straight line. 'Save your sympathy, mademoiselle. The legend is just a charming fairytale.'

'Why do you say that?' Jenna was stung by his sudden withdrawal. 'Such a fairytale was once real life! Lord's son enjoys affair with innkeeper's daughter, and goes to war. The baby dies. The girl hears of his impending marriage. She always knew it must be so. But she's devastated!' An uncanny sense of empathy crept into her heart. Unaware that her face was reflecting the dark emotions of another age, she willed him to step with her into the past.

'You think she should not believe news of his betrothal, but wait . . . until he returned from battle, laden with . . . ?' He stopped.

'Treasure!' Comprehension sparked Jenna's eyes to fire. 'So that's why you don't want reporters here — especially those who look under stones. You think they're casing the joint!'

Flinging back his head, Luc roared with laughter. His strong white teeth and tanned throat turned Jenna's limbs to water. 'Casing the joint! I must refresh my knowledge of your language!'

More seriously he said, 'You must have heard, even seen for yourself, that this estate has financial problems. Problems which a long-ago treasure would certainly solve,' he added wryly. 'I am sorry to disappoint you but there is none.' The grooves beside his mouth deepened and his eyes were sombre. 'These myths are appealing. But I cannot bear to have the deaths of my father and brother sensationalised.' His look was direct. 'I apologise for the rudeness I have shown you. But you must agree — it is reasonable to suspect beautiful women who could prise confidences from my nephew!'

A note of constraint was still there. And it troubled her.

When she returned to the Auberge des Fleurs, Elspeth, looking ten years younger, was replacing the telephone receiver.

'The hospital says that Philippe might be allowed home next week!'

Her happiness infected everyone that evening, and Jenna was glad to forget trouble for a while. She went to bed in good spirits, but her sleep was disturbed by visions of a man with green eyes, eyes which briefly looked at her — and seemed to like what they saw.

3

Morning brought a fresh problem. The ice-making machine had flooded. Muttering under his breath, Arnaud stepped gingerly over a puddle which had gathered between two uneven flagstones. 'What imbecile turned off the switch?' he stormed.

Today, however, nothing could blight Elspeth's mood, as she looked forward to Philippe's return. She began preparations for tonight. The council had booked the hotel's modest function room for a meeting with traders from nearby towns, followed by dinner. This reservation would bring welcome income, opportunity to advertise the restaurant, and encourage them to return with friends and families during the quiet winter months.

Jenna mopped up the water, against a background of Arnaud's grumbles. She sympathised with the chef. The kitchen was his domain, over which he presided with military precision. No one admitted to accidentally switching off the machine, although he dropped dark hints about Suzette.

More troubles came. Their fruit and vegetable delivery should have arrived an hour ago. Arnaud telephoned the suppliers, his face reddening until colour tinged his bald head. He slammed down the receiver.

'The girl swears that we telephoned to cancel!' he roared. 'They can bring nothing! Their van has already departed. It will not return for hours!'

'How could they make such a mistake?' Elspeth's voice rose. 'We've scarcely enough for lunch, let alone the council dinner!' Slamming down her knife, she marched from the kitchen.

Ten minutes later, the door almost left its hinges as, flushed and tight-lipped, she flung it wide. 'They say that I spoke to Henri Tournon.' She raked her fingers through her hair, till it looked as if it had been swept by a hurricane. 'He was embarrassed, but adamant.'

Arnaud and Jenna exchanged unhappy glances. Unconsciously, Arnaud glanced at the ice-making machine.

Elspeth struck the table, scattering cutlery. 'I know what you're thinking. But I haven't lost my mind!'

'Let's jot down everything we need,' suggested Jenna quickly, 'If I hurry, I should catch the market at Lamache.'

Within minutes, she was on her way in their aged run-about. At the market canopied tables held melons, peaches and oranges alongside the warm reds and vibrant greens of aubergines, peppers, lettuce, beans and broccoli.

Her favourite pavement café beckoned from across the square. Beneath a blue and green striped awning, she sighted Robert and Rachel Selwyn. They were with a dark-haired man, and didn't notice Jenna. He was probably a bookseller, she guessed, negotiating a deal. Amused, she decided 'haggling' was a better description, to judge from their absorbed faces. She'd better not interrupt. In any case, there was no time to linger.

Reaching home, after a quiet lunch-time Elspeth and Arnaud were amicably discussing a revised menu. The three of them worked hard in the kitchen during the afternoon. Preparations for the evening were almost complete when Jenna recalled her promise to Guy the previous day.

'My binoculars!' Frantically, Guy's eyes had searched the chateau kitchen. 'I dropped them when I fell!'

'I will find them,' his uncle had reassured, ruffling the child's hair. 'They are the ones Papa gave you, are they not?'

Guy had swallowed hard. 'I used them to watch for boats on the river. Then I wanted to explore the old walls. And that is when I slipped.'

Jenna had been intrigued to witness this tenderness in the man. Was she the only person to whom he presented a façade of Arctic ice? Antarctic actually, because that went deeper!

She had offered to fetch the binoculars. 'It will be best if I go,' she'd told Luc de Villiers. 'I know where Guy fell. I'll bring them back tomorrow.'

Reluctantly he had agreed. 'It seems once more you place us in your debt.'

With this evening's meal under control, Jenna could be spared for an hour.

'Be careful,' Elspeth warned. 'Those ruins look solid but, in reality, they're an accident waiting to happen.'

Jenna nodded. 'I'll watch what I'm doing,' she promised. 'Never fear, Auntie dear!' She dodged a well-aimed dishcloth and went off, chuckling.

It was easy to locate the ruined building where Guy had fallen, because one of its chimneys still stood, an ivy-clad finger thrusting upwards. Once the village bakery, it had been destroyed a century ago in a devastating rockfall. Clambering over the walls, she reached the cleft. The region was honeycombed with such crevices. Perhaps it was lucky that Guy had caught his ankle before he went farther, or rescue might have been a lot more difficult.

She quickly sighted the binoculars. They weren't a toy, but functional yet still light-weight. Hugo de Villiers had chosen well for the son who was so touchingly mature for his years.

As she entered the courtyard of the chateau, her footsteps automatically slowed. The statue seemed to beckon. Drawing closer, Jenna looked up at the lonely figure. 'Poor girl! If only you'd known how much Marcel loved you.' The sun dipped behind a cloud, casting shade across the smooth marble features.

She found Guy in a sunny recess at the side of the building, his injured ankle bandaged and propped up on a stool. The small table at his elbow held a cluttered selection of books and coloured pencils but, yet again, he was alone.

'Hi there!' she said brightly.

His face lit, his smile widening as, laughingly, she hid the binoculars

45

behind her back, before handing them to him.

'Thank you, thank you!'

'Exactly. Thank you, thank you!' The deep voice of his uncle echoed his.

As usual, Luc de Villiers wasn't smiling, although his attitude had eased marginally since their first encounter. His eyes were appraising Jenna.

She knew he was still unwilling to trust her. Even so, she found herself wishing that for once — just once! — he could see her wearing something other than serviceable jeans and workaday top. Anxious not to disappoint Guy, she'd only briefly checked her appearance before hurrying to find his binoculars. She had no idea that her silver-grey eyes, sun-dusted cheeks and pale golden hair made her beautiful no matter what she wore.

'I beg your pardon?' Embarrassed, she realised he had been speaking.

'I was telling you that Guy's mother, my sister-in-law, arrives tomorrow for a short holiday. Guy has told her that you are his good angel.' Was Luc de Villiers laughing at her again? 'Madeleine has asked to meet you, to thank you for your kindness to her son.'

'Please, Mademoiselle Jenna, come to dinner with us?' pleaded Guy.

'As Guy requests, please, Mademoiselle Jenna, will you dine with us one evening this week?' At last the stern lips relaxed, confirming that, incredibly, he was teasing her. 'We realise that your presence is invaluable at the Auberge des Fleurs but perhaps your aunt can manage without you for one evening?'

Jenna soon left, having committed herself to dine at the chateau two days later. As she passed the marble nymph, who still kept solitary vigil inside the battlements, she asked 'What do you think of that? Inn-keeper's niece dining with the lord's family. How times change — I wish you could come too!' Was it imagination, or did the wistful face warm slightly, become a half-smile?

★   ★   ★

Madeleine de Villiers, Guy's mother, turned out to be a charming and elegant Parisienne. Petite and dark-haired, her gratitude was obviously genuine. Unconsciously, she echoed Jenna's thoughts.

'He is too much alone — and so he finds danger,' she said, leading Jenna into a softly-lit salon and offering an aperitif.

'Poor Luc has so much to deal with — his own business and now the affairs of my husband and father-in-law. He cannot find time also to amuse a child.'

Seated beside the huge fireplace, she stared into the flames. 'Hugo and I built our computer company from nothing and I had to attend a conference in Italy at the start of Guy's school holidays. It was unavoidable.' Sensing Jenna's understanding, she admitted, 'International contacts are even more important since Hugo's death.' It seemed that Elspeth was right in thinking that the de Villiers family had little money to spare.

Guy was cheerfully resigned to the

fact that he could not join the adults for dinner. His ankle had mended quickly and he now walked with hardly a limp.

'In ten minutes it will be bed-time!' Madeleine kissed his cheek. Before saying goodnight, he graphically described his accident. Madeleine was an appreciative audience, exclaiming and gasping with dismay. A sideways twinkle confirmed that she'd heard it several times before.

Still laughing, Jenna was able to greet Luc de Villiers with seeming confidence as he entered the room. With him came another woman, who was introduced as Madeleine's sister.

Simone was of medium height, her slim figure revealing slight but shapely curves beneath her short black evening dress. Styled by an expert, her chestnut hair was designed to enhance her slender neck and small, pearl-studded ears.

The sisters wore their sophistication as discreetly as kid gloves and Jenna was pleasantly surprised to find that conversation with them flowed easily and was good-humoured.

It helped also that, although less expensively clothed than Madeleine and Simone, she knew she looked her best. Her grey silk dress, with its long sleeves and Empire-line bodice, was plain but well-cut. With it she wore high-heeled silver sandals and Elspeth had loaned her a short, delicate silver chain on which hung a small bell.

'With your fair hair and grey eyes you look like gossamer — as though you might float on the slightest puff of wind!'

In the dining room, Madame Dupont was hovering, ready to serve dinner. She exchanged a conspiratorial smile with Jenna as if to say 'My! You're coming up in the world!' Jenna, hiding her amusement, accepted her new role as the housekeeper's protégée.

Thick, albeit faded, tapestry curtains hung at the windows and branched candlesticks lit the long, polished table. The dinner service was old and probably valuable but on the stone walls she noticed outlines where large paintings had hung at one time. Presumably the old lord had disposed of them, in order to prop up his crumbling estate.

Simone had guessed Jenna's thoughts.

'When Luc has made the chateau rich again, he will locate the original paintings and replace them on the walls. Is that not so, cheri?' She arched a finely-traced eyebrow at the man who sat, with the unconscious arrogance of his noble ancestry, at the head of the table.

'And how do you suggest that Luc should make the chateau rich again?' In spite of his teasing tone, his expression was far warmer than any he'd directed at Jenna, she realised dismally.

'When we find Marcel's treasure, of course!' As Luc's face turned to stone, Simone clapped a scarlet-tipped hand to her mouth. 'Pardon! Je m'excuse!' Contrite, she touched Luc's arm. 'I know you prefer that we do not talk of this. But,' she gestured charmingly towards Jenna, 'we are with friends.'

That was a description which Luc de Villiers didn't apply to his dinner guest, Jenna realised, acutely embarrassed. Until now, he had been a solicitous, urbane host. Now, the familiar ice returned, a frost which she thought unfairly directed towards her, since it was Simone who had been indiscreet!

Madeleine came to Jenna's rescue.

'I'm sure Jenna realises that we prefer not to speak of the old legend. There was so much intrusion from the media when the accident happened. But of course, it would be wonderful if such a tale were true!'

'I know little about the story except that Marcel was deeply in love with the innkeeper's daughter. Does anyone know her name?' Jenna looked from one sister to the other, hoping to draw conversation away from the treasure.

'Celestine.' Madeleine glanced at Luc, whose black brows were still drawn in a straight line. In an obvious effort to lighten the atmosphere, she lifted the wine decanter and smilingly indicated Jenna's glass. When Jenna shook her head, Madeleine took a sip from her own glass before continuing. 'The legend is what the English would call the stuff of romance, similar to your tales of Nottingham Forest and Robin Hood.'

Simone, recovering from her faux pas, tried to make amends. 'The path of Richard Coeur de Lion is strewn with tales of treasure, beautiful women and daring, heroic causes.'

'Also with bloodstained acquisition and defeat!' Luc reminded her. His face softened slightly as he turned his dark head towards Simone. Jenna wasn't surprised. Madeleine's sister was attractive and immaculately groomed, the sort of woman he was accustomed to. What was worse, she recognised, Simone was immensely likeable!

'You must not spoil our fun, cheri! My sister and I like to pretend that Marcel rode home, laden with riches!' Simone's words were light but long eyelashes hid her expression as she began to slice a peach.

Jenna knew the other woman was trying to undo any damage. A few days earlier, Luc had dismissed as fantasy Jenna's notion of treasure. Tonight she knew the truth: that he believed something of value was concealed in the chateau. Admittedly, she was a stranger but she'd hoped they were growing to like and trust her. Their effort to re-impose a barrier was unexpected — and surprisingly hurtful.

Although conversation became general again she longed for the evening to end. When Madeleine asked about her work, she was tempted to resent their intrusion into her private life, but forced herself to talk about her tiny characters' adventures. Soon, the sisters were chuckling as she described how Guy had found her sitting on the ground with Albert and Oswald Ant. A glint of humour even passed over Luc's saturnine features. Without seeming impolite, Jenna managed to avoid meeting his eyes. She couldn't pretend. He had lied to her. Perhaps he'd already forgotten how, careless of her feelings, he'd shut her out of their intimate circle — but Jenna hadn't.

Or maybe he had remembered, and was trying to make amends when he suggested that she might borrow a book from the chateau's library.

'Hugo often used it to identify his specimens. There are superb engravings of insects which would interest you. I am sure that Madeleine would not object.'

'It is an excellent suggestion!' Madeleine reassured Jenna, who was still taken aback by Luc's changed mood. 'When we were here, Hugo spent hours in the library or would ramble the countryside and return laden with plants and, inevitably, a jar of insects. In that respect, Guy certainly takes after his father.'

She looked at Jenna. 'Luc and I had warned Guy not to poke around the ruined cottages, but I remember Hugo doing exactly that the day before he died.' Her eyes were sad, despite a reminiscent smile. 'He was particularly happy that evening, pulling out maps and plans of St. Justin. He said that he intended to investigate a whole new insect world.' The smile twisted.

Luc rose and placed a comforting hand on Madeleine's shoulder as she pushed back her chair.

'I will fetch the book now,' he said, watching Jenna stand. Then he added, as though unable to help himself; 'My brother would have enjoyed meeting you.'

Despising herself for the tingle of pleasure she experienced, Jenna made a noncommittal answer. His eyes narrowed as he registered her restraint. Briefly, his fingers gripped her arm as they left the dining room. Almost immediately, he withdrew his hand, but the sensation of his touch lingered.

★　★　★

Later, as she drove from the chateau, Jenna let out a long sigh. She was

56

dangerously attracted to Luc de Villiers and it must stop. The evening had been like the curate's egg — good in parts. But the net result was negative.

Luc had escorted her to where she had left her car. Moonlight was filtered by a passing cloud and hid his expression as he told her to drive carefully.

'Your aunt cannot afford more mishaps.'

'What do you mean?' Jenna's voice was sharp. She sensed his surprise.

His teeth glinted. 'You have forgotten my own personal newspaper.'

'Oh! Madame Dupont!' Of course, she should have remembered that the housekeeper's incredible network of friends would enable her to relay the spiciest items of news.

Negligently, Luc raised a hand as Jenna started the engine. In the rear view mirror she noticed him wait until she rounded the bend, but then she could no longer see him.

The track twisted in hairpin bends to the main street. The final loop was particularly tight. As she slowed, Jenna had an unrestricted view along the pavement which led to the Auberge des Fleurs. Two people were walking quickly in her direction. Before the full glare of her headlights could reach them, they dodged into a recess where steps led up to the fountain.

As she drew to a halt beside the hotel, Jenna wondered. Why was Suzette anxious not to be seen with Claude Jalabert? Or was it Claude who didn't want to be identified? The night was bright enough for Jenna to recognize the young man whose father owned the other hotel in St Justin. Auguste Jalabert was perhaps too charming to be sincere, but he was pleasant enough. The Coq d'Or was larger and more luxurious than the Auberge des Fleurs. When Philippe's father died ten years ago, Auguste had offered to purchase the smaller hotel, but respected Philippe's decision to continue his parent's business.

As for Suzette — Jenna didn't particularly like the girl; but there appeared to be no reason for the couple to keep their romance secret. Unless, of course, it didn't suit Auguste's plans for his son.

Switching off the engine, she frowned as niggling doubts crowded back. Recently Auguste had again offered to buy the Auberge des Fleurs. It seemed beyond coincidence that, at the same time, a Paris lawyer, on behalf of unknown clients, was pressing Philippe to sell. Even Robert Selwyn had joked that he fancied himself as an hotelier.

'Our daughter could run the place.' He'd met Elspeth's sceptical eyes with an innocent smile. 'I'm seriously tempted.' His smile broadened. 'What d'you think of a secondhand bookstall — on your patio, perhaps?'

Shaking her head, Jenna struggled to clear the tangled web. Something was wrong, but she couldn't pinpoint what that something was.

All was quiet when she entered the tiled reception area. Elspeth had given the few overnight guests their own keys in case they wished to return late. Softly welcoming, an ornate pewter lamp illuminated the stairs and landing.

And then Jenna noticed a shaft of light beyond Philippe's office. It came from the one-time storage space which was now her bedroom. She had locked the door, but it swung open at her touch.

'No!' She gasped when she saw the inside of her room. The intruder had done his work thoroughly. He'd upturned her wardrobe and dressing table, wrenched the mirror from the wall and slung it amongst shattered glass from two Chagall prints which Jenna loved. The drawers which held her clothes hung half-open but their contents seemed untouched. What madness was this?

Turning, she tripped over the red Oriental rug, heaved aside on the stone floor. She grabbed at the door jamb, and then hesitated. Upstairs, her aunt would be sleeping. They would have to call the police eventually. But, first, Jenna needed to think. Who could have done this? And why?

Her limbs turned to water. She sank onto the edge of her bed, realising with cold dread that danger hung like a stifling mist, over the Auberge des Fleurs.

4

There was no way of hiding what had happened and early in the morning, Jenna showed Elspeth, who rushed to telephone the gendarmerie. Jenna caught sight of Suzette at the open door. The girl scuttled away when she realised she'd been seen.

Even Arnaud's usual hearty roar dropped to a whisper. 'Why do they wreck only this one small room?'

Elspeth returned. 'They'll come within the hour.' Today, as they waited for the police, she looked every year of her age. 'I'm so sorry, love! Are you certain nothing was stolen?'

'Not a thing! That's what's so weird.' Jenna's perplexed eyes surveyed the chaos. She had dozed uneasily in an armchair in the lounge, her eyes flying open at the smallest sound. All her doubts had gone. Someone was desperate for Elspeth and Philippe to leave.

But why tear her room apart? Why not the office? The bedroom furniture was cumbersome. So there was more than one intruder. If they hadn't come to steal, their sole aim must be to wear Elspeth down until she persuaded Philippe to sell.

There was no sign that they'd been in other rooms and the overnight guests had said nothing. Elspeth was careful to serve their breakfasts personally. She sent Suzette on an errand and, with unwarranted optimism, warned her to say nothing to anyone on the way.

But soon, Bertrand stamped into the kitchen, black eyes flashing fire.

'What madman has wrecked my stores?' he shouted.

They followed him to the stone outhouse which jutted from the rear of the hotel. Inside, the overflowing ledges had been stripped bare and boxes, sacks, Bertrand's tools were slung everywhere. The massive shelves which had felled Mr. Selwyn teetered precariously beneath a jumble of paintpots, bottles and other maintenance equipment.

Two gendarmes arrived. They made notes, advised Elspeth to take extra precautions with security, didn't stay long and offered little reassurance. Frustrated, Elspeth reminded them that there was still no explanation for the rockfall which might have killed Philippe.

The sergeant's face was sombre as he scanned the painted shutters and the wrought-iron lanterns that hung above the arched entrance of the building.

'Be assured, madame, our investigations continue — your husband's accident remains an open file.'

Later that morning, they received an unexpected visit from Auguste Jalabert. A short, snowy-haired man, his fleshy jowls betrayed a love of good food and he had the benevolent air of a Santa Claus. Following him came Claude, whose stringy frame, narrow forehead and jaunty step provided a bizarre contrast.

Auguste seemed genuinely concerned. He had heard about the break-in because, he said, with a look of mock resignation, the village grapevine was already active. As far as Jenna was concerned, his condolences were more suited to a bereavement. A sleepless night had left her jangled nerves ready to analyse every word, every shade of expression.

'Perhaps, madame, you and your husband will now decide that St Justin and hotel-keeping are not for you.' Nothing could be more avuncular than Auguste's gentle pat on Elspeth's hand.

Elspeth shook her head.

'We thrive on trouble, Monsieur Jalabert!' she said cheerfully. 'My husband will soon be home, we shall have a good tourist season, and these incidents will be forgotten.' Jenna could only admire her aunt's desire to bluff the opposition.

'I applaud your courage.' If Auguste felt frustrated, he was careful not to show it. He tapped the side of his nose meaningfully. 'But do not forget that I can offer you a good price. My son,' he waved an arm towards Claude, who was silently prowling the room, with no apparent interest in the conversation, 'will need his own business when he marries. He and his wife will be glad of a little help from Papa Auguste.' A chesty laugh rumbled through his frame. 'Especially when les enfants arrive!'

'Is your son planning to marry soon?' Elspeth asked politely.

Jenna was noting the expression on Claude's face. Rather like a cornered rat she decided, and wondered if Suzette was listening at the door. Normally she would have chuckled quietly at Claude's plight, but not today.

Again, Auguste laughed.

'Let us say that his father has plans for him . . . and, like a good son, Claude always listens to good advice.'

Jenna doubted whether Suzette featured in Auguste's schemes. The girl wasn't the sort of match that the hotelier would encourage. She fitted neither his social nor financial aspirations for his only son.

Elspeth heaved a sigh of relief as the door closed behind them.

'Auguste is certainly persistent,' she said. 'But, if Philippe and I did decide to sell, we'd prefer the new owners to be strangers, or from another local family. Healthy competition is always best, especially in a small village like this. If Claude became manager, he'd be dominated by his father. The Auberge des Fleurs would be a satellite of the Coq d'Or and lose all of its unique flavour.'

Jenna agreed. She couldn't help wondering if Claude was serious about Suzette, and keeping his intentions secret until Auguste had purchased a second business. That would explain his wish not to be seen last night. On the other hand, ambition had sharpened his features. He'd recognise the drawbacks of marriage to such a socially inadequate girl — but that wouldn't stop him from playing around with her.

Later, sitting in her favourite spot beside the fountain, Jenna's thoughts returned to the person, or persons, who had vandalised her room. Today, even her sketchpad and pencils failed to work their usual magic. Had it been Claude? He might be trying to frighten and pressurise Elspeth, either for his father or on his own behalf. He and Suzette had come from the direction of the Auberge des Fleurs last night; they hadn't wanted to be seen . . . maybe he'd sweet-talked the girl into helping him?

But what if it was another person from the village? Someone who bore Philippe malice? They had turned her room upside down, but taken nothing. As Jenna stared into space, she saw nothing of any help, only questions, their answers shrouded in fog.

'Lateral thinking.' The words popped into her head. She smiled. This was her father's approach when he faced seemingly insurmountable problems. For a moment, she longed for the comforting presence of her parents.

'Okay Dad!' Settling herself more comfortably, and closing her eyes, she murmured 'Let's try some lateral thinking.'

Slowly, her reflections began to follow a different route. Whoever was behind this, they were getting desperate. Elspeth and Philippe had shown no sign of selling, despite everything that had gone wrong.

Her room had once been part of Bertrand's outhouse. In fact, the heavy door connecting the two still remained, normally concealed behind her wardrobe.

Her heart began to beat faster as realisation dawned. Whoever it was, they didn't want the hotel. They wanted something that was inside it!

She half-rose, ready to rush back and search every inch of her room. Then she stopped. What did she expect to find, for goodness' sake? For the moment, all she could do was wait and keep watch.

With a huge effort, Jenna forced herself to think of other things. She would need a clear head when the next trouble came — and that it would come, she was completely certain.

★   ★   ★

At first, it was a relief to turn her mind to Luc de Villiers and his family. Madeleine and Simone were women with whom she could enjoy spending time, despite the differences in their background and lifestyle. From snippets of conversation across the dinner table, she'd guessed that their parents held a respected position amongst the old and impoverished French aristocracy, similar to the de Villiers dynasty. Simone, like her sister, had a demanding career, not surprisingly in the fashion industry, which explained why she'd been unable to care for Guy while Madeleine was abroad.

As for Luc — he was an intriguing mixture. He took responsibility for his family, was attached to his sister-in-law, and loving towards his nephew.

Jenna's musings came to a halt. She preferred not to remember how Simone had placed her slim white fingers on his arm. They knew each other well, and it showed. Sharing mutual interests and sophisticated city life, they'd make a good-looking couple.

Did Jenna, the girl from the village inn, ever enter Luc's mind? She was the modern-day equivalent of Celestine, she supposed dispiritedly. Whereas he, of course, was like Marcel, charismatic and proud, son of the lord. Uneasily she recognised the danger of making such comparisons. Luc de Villiers would never fall for Jenna Edwards. He'd never share with her the depth of love that Marcel and Celestine had known — a love which had eventually destroyed them both.

Telling herself not to be a fool, Jenna picked up her pad and started to sketch a caterpillar as it made leisurely progress across a corner of the fountain.

An hour later, and reluctantly because the air felt clean and beautiful and the hotel held uneasy vibrations, she wandered back along the path. There was work to be done. The restaurant might be busy on a Saturday evening.

At the junction where steps led to the street, she heard her name called. Looking back, she was surprised to see the Selwyns descending the narrow track above.

'Jenna! Hello there!' She liked Robert Selwyn. Easy to talk to, and always interesting, he loved reminiscing about historians and their written histories.

'Your aunt mentioned that you dined at the chateau last night.' Rachel Selwyn was unexpectedly affable, especially since, after her husband's accident, she had remained distant.

'Yes, I had a very enjoyable evening,' Jenna lied. 'The chateau is centuries old, of course.'

'So we understand.' Robert's eyes were bright as he polished his spectacles with a handkerchief. His interest in the past extended far beyond his collection of antiquarian books. Jenna knew that the couple spent hours inside churches and ancient buildings, scouring every detail of their origins. With a sinking heart, she anticipated his request, silently wishing that Elspeth had said nothing.

'Is there a chance that you could persuade your friends to allow us a look inside? Not the private rooms, of course,' he added hastily. 'Just the main hall and the library, perhaps?'

'We should be so grateful,' added his wife. Almost as tall as her husband, she appeared more approachable today, perhaps because her hairstyle and her expression were less severe, decided Jenna. She must have been quite the stunner in her younger years.

Jenna had no wish to approach Luc de Villiers on their behalf. She had a shrewd idea what his answer would be.

'I'm afraid I can't pretend to know the family well.'

A voice came from behind her.

'On the contrary, Jenna, you are highly regarded as our friend.'

Luc stood slightly below her on the steps, having ascended from the street. His green eyes held a malicious glint as he glanced at her, before greeting her companions with his attractive smile.

'You will pardon me, madame and monsieur. I thank you for your interest in my family home. I am Luc de Villiers.' His eyes returned to Jenna, but now they held concern as he noted her unusual pallor and the strain which she couldn't hide. 'Perhaps Jenna would be kind enough to complete the introduction.'

What a snake! Jenna's scowl was hidden from the Selwyns, but Luc's smile deepened as she was obliged to introduce them.

Within minutes, he had invited the English couple to visit the chateau the following day. They accepted with delight and were equally pleased when Luc suggested that they should continue along the upper path and at the end, inspect a low wall behind the fountain.

'You will find a most unusual inscription there. I shall look forward to hearing what you think of it.'

With a few masterly strokes, Jenna acknowledged later, he had not only pleased the Selwyns but also dismissed them and, with a light touch on her elbow, maneouvred Jenna into a walk with him beside the river.

⋆ ⋆ ⋆

'I have just spoken with your aunt,' Luc said conversationally, although he retained a light grip on Jenna's elbow. He was wise to suspect that she'd cut and run, she thought. Her heart said, 'Stay, talk, enjoy being with him,' but common-sense warned she mustn't let him take up permanent residence there.

She said nothing. He bent slightly to examine her expressionless face. His mouth quirked, although his eyes were serious. 'I apologise for taking you from your friends, but I wanted some time alone with you.'

Her heart lurched briefly and then steadied. Could he hear it beating? 'They're not my friends.' She kicked herself. What an inane response! In carefully neutral tones she asked 'Is Guy all right?'

Luc nodded his head. 'My nephew is enjoying his holiday, especially now that his mother and his aunt are here.' He steered Jenna closer to the water, where a track led towards the distant bridge. There was room for them to walk beside each other, although his arm brushed hers as he adapted his stride.

'The only problem we need to discuss is the Auberge des Fleurs. I am concerned that it has seen two potentially fatal accidents, and now a burglary — all within the space of a few weeks. If you had disturbed the intruders, you might have been attacked, even killed!'

'Is that why you came looking for me?' Jenna could hardly believe her ears. Why on earth should Luc de Villiers interest himself in her misfortunes?

He hesitated, as though unsure of the answer. Finally, he let out a long sigh.

'I am concerned for your aunt and uncle, of course. Even more, I look at you and I see the chateau's nymph — finely-wrought, loyal, with strength to forge her own destiny. And yet so vulnerable.'

Jenna's eyes widened. Her spirits took wing as she tried to absorb what he had just said.

After a moment, he continued. 'Madame Dupont was quick to tell me that, on returning home last night, you found your room had been totally ransacked.'

She nodded, still bemused. Did he really see in her something of the beautiful, tragic Celestine? Realising that he was waiting, she forced herself to speak. 'They didn't steal anything. All they did was create havoc — not only in my bedroom, but in Bertrand's storehouse, too.'

When she glanced at Luc, a little shyly, his eyes were seemingly focussed on a series of ripples where fish swam close to the surface. When he spoke, his attractively accented tones sent liquid fire through her veins, even as his words tugged her back to reality.

'Jenna, you must tell me every incident which has created trouble for your aunt and uncle. Even the smallest, from the moment you found reason to come to help them.'

It was hard to know where to start. Obviously he'd heard of the most extreme happenings. But how could she relate those which seemed trivial until, when added together, they threatened to destroy everything that Elspeth and Philippe had achieved?

Luc understood her dilemma. 'You can speak freely.' A corner of his mouth lifted in what might have been self-mockery. 'In the absence of your uncle, I believe that the de Villiers family must look after their own — in this case, the women who keep alive St Justin's oldest inn.'

It was a put-down which obliterated every vestige of the warmth he had generated minutes earlier. Now, the glow turned to cinders. He'd made his position brutally plain, perhaps deliberately. The de Villiers family honoured their 'feudal obligation' to those who lived beneath the chateau. 'Beneath' wasn't a matter of location, Jenna realised bleakly. To Luc, it represented the distinction between 'upstairs' lord and 'downstairs' innkeepers.

'It's kind of you to be concerned for us,' she struggled to distance herself. 'But there's absolutely no need. My uncle's accident was unfortunate but, luckily, I was free to help my aunt. In any case, he'll be home soon and things will get back to normal.'

'And last night's intrusion?'

'Mindless vandalism. Nothing more.'

Luc halted, blocking the path, so that Jenna was obliged to stop. Gripping her shoulders, he swung her to face him.

His keen eyes took in the purple shadows under her lowered lids, and the near-colourless lips that showed no trace of their usual humour.

'Jenna.' A note of warning made her look up into a dark scrutiny that was stern, but not unkind. 'I mean to discover whether these events are related, or mere coincidence. You will start at the beginning, please. And you will not stop until you reach the end.'

He didn't move, and his expression made it clear that he wouldn't let her leave. Mortified that she'd misread his concern — and that he might have noticed — she felt a surge of resentment. He would be frantic with worry if it was Simone whose room was wrecked, and equally upset if anything affected Madeleine.

But by stark contrast, bottom of the list, came the almost feudal duty he felt towards her — the troublesome little English girl and her awkward family.

Mutinously she planted her feet in an attitude of defiance and pressed her lips together. They stood, neither prepared to give in. But Luc was bigger than her. His sinewy limbs were strong, his grip firm. Eventually Jenna had to accept the fact that, if she wanted to get home tonight, she must accept defeat.

'Okay then,' she said ungraciously. 'My uncle's accident happened when he was sitting in his usual place on the patio. He loves the fresh air and often takes his paperwork outdoors on quiet days.'

Momentarily she paused, picturing the tranquillity of the scene. Then, forgetting the man who stood listening, she spread her hands helplessly. 'Some boulders fell on him. It can't have been an accident, because there was no overhanging rock.' The image of Philippe's pain was as clear as the vision of her aunt's anxious features.

'When I arrived, Aunt Elspeth told me they'd been worried about a spate of cancellations, and that surprisingly generous offers had come from people wanting to buy them out.'

'And what then?' he encouraged.

She shrugged, hoping that he wouldn't laugh at her.

'Oh, silly things. Someone switched off the ice-making machine and flooded the kitchen. An important grocery order was cancelled by someone pretending to be my aunt.' Tears rose in her throat. Head bent, she scuffed the ground with the toe of her trainer. It was a relief to share her fears, but hearing her voice putting those fears into words was appalling. She dare not ignore the implications. Deliberate harm had been attempted. What might happen next?

When she raised her head, Luc saw that her long dark lashes were wet. 'My uncle could have died. And when a wooden dresser toppled, it could have killed one of our guests!'

'But it did not.' Almost absentmindedly Luc was holding her shoulders again, but this time his touch soothed as it moved downwards to her elbows.

Jenna scarcely noticed. She was

recalling Robert Selwyn's terrifying stillness. 'He was very shaken and his wife went ballistic. I don't blame her. She, of course, blamed my aunt. Said the furniture was old and unsafe.'

'And was it?'

Jenna shook her head, and said honestly: 'Old, yes. Unsafe, no. Unless someone gave a hearty shove from the alcove behind it.'

'And that is what you suspect?'

Her unhappy grey eyes gave Luc his answer.

They started walking again, each wrapped in their private thoughts. The silence was companionable but was eventually broken by Luc. Hands casually in the pockets of his brown suede jacket, he could have been mistaken for a holiday-maker. A closer look, however, would have made them wonder the reason for the furrows between his brows and beside his mouth.

'If these acts were deliberate, have you any suspicions as to who might be behind them?'

Again she shook her head. 'Not really. Some lawyer in Paris is apparently acting for a would-be purchaser, and Auguste Jalabert is keen to buy the business for his son.'

'But these advances are reasonable, do you not think? The lawyer might be acting for a client who has seen the Auberge des Fleurs, finds the building and its location attractive, and hopes for a profitable investment. Auguste's interest is understandable. But would he really stoop to the kind of underhand methods such as you describe?'

Luc wasn't disputing her fears, Jenna knew, feeling a modicum of comfort. He was merely ticking off possibilities.

'I can't believe that Auguste would do anything criminal,' she said slowly. 'On the other hand, his son might be keen to get the business as a wedding present.' She described how Claude and Suzette had scurried into the darkness last night, avoiding Jenna's headlights. Luc raised his eyebrows in disbelief.

'I know the girl slightly. Surely she would not appeal to Claude Jalabert? He is quite a worldly young man. The girl spent a week working at the chateau. This was several years ago, when I happened to be in St Justin.' Amusement fanned the tiny lines beside his eyes. 'I remember that Madame Dupont could not wait to see her go!'

Jenna's mouth curved. The house-keeper was good-hearted and would have tried to help the girl by giving her a job. But Madame Dupont's tongue was sharp, her movements brisk. It would have been an impossible partner-ship!

Luc echoed Jenna's speculation about the relationship between Claude and Suzette. He, too, wondered if the girl was being manipulated. 'Suzette is familiar with the routine of your hotel. She could be a most useful accomplice if he wished to cause mischief.'

'Yes. Whether or not Claude has honourable intentions towards her is a big question.' Opening her mouth to say more, Jenna closed it again, her teeth worrying her bottom lip.

Luc noticed. 'There is more that troubles you, I think.'

Jenna didn't know how to go on. How could she confess her crazy notion that it wasn't the building that their tormenter wanted, but something it contained? He would think this the stuff of fantasy!

Mistaking her reticence, Luc frowned slightly but obviously decided that he'd probed enough for one day. Slowing, he turned and didn't press her to say any more. Jenna sensed his withdrawal but the moment for more confidences had passed. By now, they had almost reached the stone-built bridge which spanned the waters before they flowed onwards to the next village. From here, as they retraced their steps, the chateau was bathed in light from the late afternoon sun.

'How beautiful it looks!' Impulsively Jenna held out her arm, as if she would like to caress its mellow stones. 'I can understand how you and your family love your home so much.'

'That is true. We feel privileged to be part of its history.' His laugh was short and rueful. 'But that privilege carries a price.'

'A financial price, I imagine,' she hazarded.

'One that will rest heavily on Guy's shoulders when he is older. His mother is fighting to keep Hugo's business afloat, but even that will provide less revenue than a drop in the ocean. The estate has been struggling with debt for years and we can see little hope of improvement.'

'Have you considered letting the building — either long-term or for holiday accommodation?' She knew there was no point even trying to suggest that it should be sold.

Luc inclined his head. 'We looked into the possibility, but the place is draughty and damp. It would take a fortune to raise it to the necessary standard.' Wryly he elaborated, 'The general public might be attracted by its romance, but they certainly wouldn't pay to live in discomfort! The rental returns would not cover the cost of refurbishment.'

Jenna was surprised that he talked so openly. In silence they continued walking, but the silence was relaxed and companionable. When they left the riverside track and returned to the main road, Luc stopped. They were so close that Jenna could feel his warm breath on her face.

'I am glad we have had time to talk. I shall think about what you have told me, and make a few enquiries. In the meantime,' his voice deepened and he touched her cheek with gentle fingers, 'I urge you to take great care.'

'I will.' Jenna tilted her head to look directly into his eyes. They were very green and seemed to hold a question. 'The police say the file is still open, but it's hard to have faith when we see no progress being made.' Sighing, she watched a lone cyclist make his way the length of the village street. 'Thank you for being concerned about us.' She started walking towards the Auberge des Fleurs.

Luc's long stride took him only a few steps before he stopped and turned.

'Jenna! One moment, if you please!'

Enquiringly, she looked over her shoulder.

'On Thursday I plan to drive my family to Limeuil, the place where the two rivers meet. You probably know it already — but the village is so beautiful that one could visit there a thousand times. I wondered if you would care to join us?'

Without thinking, she said, 'I'd love to!' After a moment's reflection, she added, 'I'd have to ask my aunt if she can spare me, but it should be alright.' Her enchanting smile brought its reward.

The flare of response in his eyes made her footsteps as light as a nymph . . .

★   ★   ★

At dinner that night, the Selwyns were joined by Sam and Oliver Hargreaves, the two geologists. Jenna wasn't surprised to hear their conversation quickly turn to the chateau. After parting with Luc earlier, she had seen them talking with the older couple on the terrace which overlooked the Auberge des Fleurs. The four had been gesticulating, sometimes towards the chateau, sometimes the medieval buildings that were wedged into every available ledge on the perpendicular rock formations.

The Hargreaves were repeating last year's visit, examining the region's caves and prehistoric remains. Both were rugged and flaxen-haired but, where Sam's was an overlong curly thatch, Oliver, the elder by a few years, had a short crop.

The Selwyns were familiar with many of the locations which interested the brothers, so conversation was lively as they demolished coq au vin and several bottles of soft red house wine.

Eventually Rachel Selwyn placed her

hand across her husband's glass.

'That's enough, Robert. We don't want one of your headaches to spoil our visit to the chateau tomorrow.'

'What's this?' asked Sam. 'The chateau isn't open to the public, is it?' A chunky man in his late thirties, his craggy features were tanned from a field trip, when he took a group of students to Turkey.

Robert Selwyn shook his head and indicated Jenna, who was clearing space for the cheese board.

'Our good fairy fixed it,' he explained. 'Rachel and I were longing to take a look inside. See if we could find more about the history of the place. There's an intriguing legend attached to it.' Responding to Sam's enquiring eyebrow, he leant closer across the candlelit table and jokingly spoke in hushed tones. 'Apparently the lord's son had a love affair with the daughter of the local inn. This place, in fact! It was a time when Richard Cöeur de Lion was recruiting men for

91

the Third Crusade.' The candles flickered, illuminating their absorbed faces. 'The young lord, Marcel de Villiers, joined him. I don't know the girl's name.'

'Celestine.'

They swung around, startled. Suzette had been hovering silently in the background. Jenna, too, was surprised. It was unusual for the waitress to speak, let alone volunteer information!

'Celestine,' mused Robert. 'I like the sound of that! Has a certain ring of romantic tragedy about it.'

'Robert! What nonsense you talk! You only say that because you know what happened to her!'

'And that was . . . ?' Oliver Hargreaves asked.

'Her baby died and she thought Marcel was to marry a rich heiress. She threw herself into the river and drowned.'

Robert turned his attention to Jenna.

'Your friend from the chateau was most amiable when he eventually joined us at the fountain. We wouldn't have noticed the wall inscription unless he'd pointed it out.' He nodded thanks as Oliver Hargreaves pushed the cheese board closer. Taking a generous helping, he reached for the biscuits and butter.

'Unfortunately he won't be free tomorrow, but said his housekeeper would be happy to show us around.' Longingly he eyed the mouthful he was preparing. 'Would you tell him how grateful we are for our private viewing? Are you likely to see him soon?'

Unwillingly, Jenna had to tell them about Luc's invitation to visit Limeuil in two days time. She did her best to ignore Rachel Selwyn's arched expression.

'Madame de Villiers and her sister are here for a holiday. They'll have a spare seat in the car — I suppose it's a sort of thank you for helping her young son, Guy. He'd been exploring the old bakehouse when he fell into a crevice and found that he couldn't get out.'

The subject of the lord's son and the innkeeper's daughter was dropped. Conversation ranged across the world of antiquarian books, geological formations, prehistoric man in the Perigord and the glassmaking guild of medieval Venice.

For now, Celestine was forgotten.

5

It was two days later before Celestine's name again entered the conversation. This time, Jenna was in Luc de Villiers' black limousine as they headed towards Limeuil. Simone was established in the front seat when the car drew to a halt outside the Auberge des Fleurs. She greeted Jenna warmly.

'My sister sends you her apologies. Poor Madeleine! Once again she has a migraine.' Simone was clearly concerned as she described how the attacks had become more frequent since Hugo's death. 'They cause her such agony and sometimes last for several days.'

'I'm so sorry,' said Jenna. Luc had opened the rear door and was placing her beside Guy, who sat in the middle. In the far corner, to her surprise, was Madame Dupont. 'My father suffered from them until he retired. They wasted so many hours of his life. And some people think they're no more than a headache!'

As she settled herself more comfortably, Madame Dupont explained that her sister lived at Limeuil.

'When Madame de Villiers could not come because she has the malade, Monsieur suggested that I should take the opportunity to visit Agnes. She is elderly and rarely leaves her house these days. I would not have left Madame de Villiers alone, but Monsieur was adamant that she needs only quiet.'

Luc's expression was bland as he met Jenna's eyes in the driving mirror. Hurriedly, she looked down and adjusted her seat belt. It was a dangerous intimacy, this meeting of minds! Sitting back, she knew there would be little need to talk. If conversation faltered, the housekeeper would fill every gap.

Very soon Madame Dupont was describing how, yesterday, she had shown Mr. and Mrs. Selwyn the main hall and other areas inside the chateau. As Luc had helped her into the car, Jenna had already relayed their thanks to him. When she had asked if they'd enjoyed their visit, both said the interior was interesting, but hadn't elaborated. Jenna hadn't questioned them further because other guests were within earshot and she didn't want to encourage anyone else to inveigle an invitation. Perhaps the Selwyns were merely disappointed with the little they'd been shown.

She was surprised now to hear their guide's account.

'They were very interested!' Madame Dupont was so enthusiastic that Jenna couldn't help wondering the size of the tip she'd received. 'We spent a long time in the great hall where the nobles used to meet, and then they saw the drawing room and grand stairway. Outside, the keep is unsafe, so I could not let them climb. They would have lingered all day in the library, but I had work to do.'

'It was kind of you to show them around,' said Jenna. 'They're immensely interested in historical buildings.'

'You do not need to tell me that, ma petite! They wanted to know about the foundations, the building of the tower, the de Villiers family and its estate, the legend of the tragic Marcel and Celestine . . . so many questions!'

Jenna cast an apprehensive glance at the back of Luc's head. He appeared to be concentrating on the road, until Simone spoke quietly to him. Briefly he turned his head and smiled into her flawless face.

Although he had talked freely enough when they walked beside the river, Jenna knew from his reaction to Simone's blunder at the dinner party that the legend was territory which he preferred to avoid.

Madame Dupont was jumping from one topic to the next. Today, as usual, she was dressed in dark clothing, but wore her black straw hat at a rakish slant. Gleefully she announced that it would provoke acid comment from her sister, with whom she would stay overnight, returning home by bus tomorrow.

'We enjoy talking about the old days,' she told Jenna. 'Many of our childhood friends have died. But some moved away, through marriage to a stranger. It was never so in our parents' time.' She sniffed. 'Your English visitors said you have similar traditions — that in English village churchyards, as in France, one sees the same family commemorated again and again.' She tilted her head like an enquiring robin. 'Have you seen the monuments belonging to the Auberge des Fleurs?'

Jenna said that she had. She knew the ancient graveyard, situated several hundred metres behind the village, where the terrain was flat and, at this time of year, tinted green with stubby grass.

'The family tomb of Celestine is there, although the stone is worn smooth from age, of course.' Madame Dupont sniffed again, maybe to signify disapproval, or maybe sympathy, for the innkeeper's daughter. 'Her cloak was found on the riverbank. Her body was never recovered.'

'Poor girl,' murmured Jenna. 'And how terrible for her parents.' As her eyes again met Luc's in the driving mirror, she knew he was listening. It would be wise to change the subject, although how to quell the housekeeper's flow was a problem. But some inner compulsion pushed her to discover more about the girl she found so intriguing. It was as if, in some former life, she had known and liked Celestine. 'Did she have brothers and sisters?'

'One sister only, Adele, who married a man named Jean Picard. For generations their descendants worked St Justin's bakehouse. Now it lies in ruins, alas.'

'You mean the place where Guy fell?'

Madame Dupont nodded. She patted Guy's knee. He had been occupied with a wooden puzzle. Now in eight sections, once reassembled it should form a cube, he'd informed Jenna.

'So Adele lived only metres from her old home and from her sister and parents?' Jenna wrenched her eyes from the yellow daisy which, attached to the crown of the black hat, nodded with its wearer.

'It was the way of village life for centuries.'

'Until the advent of sailings to the New World, and steam,' Luc added dryly.

Madame Dupont clucked in disapproving agreement, and adjusted her hat to a truly dangerous angle. They had finally reached Limeuil. Soon she was hurrying to her sister's home.

Luc's smile was wicked as he helped Jenna from the car.

'Aren't you going to thank me for providing such absorbing on-board entertainment?' he murmured.

Pretending to frown, she quickly gave up the effort and smiled.

★   ★   ★

Limeuil enjoyed a tranquil setting. Beyond the level area of grass which sloped gently towards the bank, two stone bridges, one perpendicular to the other, spanned the confluence of the rivers Dordogne and Vezere. A man was standing waist-deep in the waters, fishing.

When Luc suggested that they walk to the hilltop park, Simone shuddered. Trim ankles, silk stockings, couture shoes with impossibly high, slender heels, didn't make for exploration on gravelled pathways, she admitted.

If she didn't like Simone so much, thought Jenna, she would be wondering the point of coming to Limeuil when you couldn't walk anywhere!

'Cheri. You know je t'adore.' Simone patted Luc's cheek. 'But I will sit at the terrace there, where one can drink excellent coffee.' She began to tiptoe towards the tea-room where tables and chairs overlooked the shady village green. She waved a hand in dismissal. 'I need to telephone my lovely Alain. So there is no need to feel guilty if you abandon me for a while.'

Luc's strong features were as relaxed as Jenna had yet seen them. He shook his head in amused resignation. 'You are a such great trial to the excellent Alain! One day you may find yourself replaced by a woman who has more than fairy dust in her head!'

Alain was Simone's boss, Jenna realised. Although she laughed at Simone's charade, she knew the man must appreciate an employee who was not only bright but beautiful and funny.

At the river bank Guy was skimming pebbles as he talked to an elderly and shaggy dog.

Luc received a final wave from Simone. 'Shall we shame her? If that is possible!' He indicated the track which led upwards between honey-tinted houses. His eyes were enjoying the delicate tint of pink on Jenna's cheeks, and the sheen of her fair hair. 'From the top you will enjoy the wonderful view, even if you have no breath to say so.'

Guy decided to join them and, to their amusement, when the dog saw the direction of their walk, he took on the role of guide. Walking a few paces in front, he led them up steps and through alleyways, always in an upwards direction.

Many of the houses and shops were shuttered until the holiday season began. Occasionally he would pause, as if to say 'Catch your breath. The outlook between those chimneys is very fine.'

The land opened into a great panorama when they reached the highest point.

'The park is closed until May,' said Luc. 'But we can visit it some other time.' Jenna said nothing but, noting her bright eyes, he seemed satisfied.

When they began to descend, again the old dog led the way. Reaching their starting point beside the two rivers, he left them without a backward glance. Smiling, they watched him go, before joining Simone for drinks and cakes.

She had been watching with amusement. 'I am not sure whether he was taking care of you, or of his beloved village.'

'Did you contact Alain?' asked Luc.

'Yes. He misses me greatly!' she said with such robust satisfaction that they all dissolved into laughter.

'There is one particular place that I want to show you,' Luc told Jenna as the car left Limeuil. 'It is the Chapelle St Martin, about one kilometre from here.' She settled back, happy that the day wasn't to end too quickly.

'The chapel was founded by Richard Coeur de Lion and Philippe II of France when they returned from the Third Crusade,' Luc explained as they wandered inside the squat little Romanesque building. Simone and Guy had briefly admired the frescoes and then gone to watch some men play boules. 'They wanted to beseech God's pardon for the murder of Thomas a'Beckett by Richard's father.'

'Will no one rid me of this turbulent priest?' quoted Jenna, recalling the disastrous words of Henry II.

Luc inclined his head. 'A tragic

outcome to a moment's fury.'

'And a lesson to be learned,' added Jenna. 'There can't be many people who have spoken in anger without regretting it afterwards.'

'Do you wish me to agree that I am one of those people?' Luc's eyes were quizzical as they suddenly held hers. The chapel was quiet.

Jenna's grey gaze was straight and clear.

'You mean that first day?' she asked bluntly.

'Yes.'

'Well, I thought you atrociously rude, of course.'

A muscle moved in his jaw but, to his credit, he didn't actually smile.

'Later, I realised why you were so suspicious of me. It didn't excuse your attitude but after such a terrible loss you must have felt indescribably raw.'

'You are very forgiving! Nevertheless, I apologise. I was objectionable and in some strange way I enjoyed — no, had a need to vent my feelings,' he interrupted Jenna's attempt to dismiss his confession.

'Madeleine and all our family were distraught. Guy, only six years old, had inherited a financial nightmare. I had to save his estate, although the problem had almost defeated my father and Hugo. I was in despair, and there was no one that I could talk to.'

His hand reached out to capture hers. Drawing her close, Luc bent his head until his breath stirred the silky tendrils of hair which fell loose today, free of their usual ponytail. 'And then you came along, sweet Jenna.'

His lips were firm and warm. They might have lingered, but a shout of triumph from the boules players reminded him that Simone and Guy were waiting outside the chapel. Before releasing Jenna, he brushed his lips across her forehead. 'You helped me, although you could not realise it, and I am grateful.'

Taking her arm, he led her into the sunshine. It was just as well that his controlling touch was there, because she had a suspicion that, with a slight puff of wind, her feet would climb up to the stars!

They stopped for a simple dinner at a restaurant where Luc, to Jenna's surprise, was obviously well known. She hadn't thought him the red-and-white checked tablecloth type. The proprietor hurried to greet him, hand outstretched.

'Monsieur, it is good to see you. Tonight we have some of your favourite fish. Or some truly magnificent steak!'

It had been a wonderful day. Heady, too, in that she sensed a new and precious intimacy between herself and Luc. Gone, at least for now, was his lord of the manor attitude towards the 'underling' from the local inn. What tomorrow held, she didn't know, but she would cherish the golden moments of today.

Dusk was falling in crimson streaks across the level lands enclosing the river. As they reached the Auberge des Fleurs, Jenna sighed contentedly. Guy was asleep and even his aunt's farewell was sleepy. That Simone and Luc had a special relationship Jenna had no doubt. But a girl could dream, couldn't she? Just for a while . . .

Luc helped her onto the pavement and raised her hand to his lips.

'Sleep well, ma cherie. Go now.' Giving her a gentle push, he waited until she reached the doorway. Then, raising one hand in his usual salute, he returned to the car and drove away.

6

Philippe returned to St Justin the following day, brought by his friend, Henri, who was keen to help in some way. 'It is best for you to show Philippe a serene face and a thriving restaurant,' he told Elspeth.

He'd chosen the wrong words for neither 'serenity' nor 'thriving' played any part in the homecoming.

'Mon Dieu! What has happened?' Philippe's eager steps halted as he entered the Auberge des Fleurs. Usually bright and welcoming, the reception area looked as though it had been hit by a cyclone. Mops and brooms had been thrown against the desk, scattering papers and flowers across the floor. That, in turn, was cluttered with buckets and saucepans — anything to hold water. Much of this had slopped, leaving a trail of dirty footprints across the tiles.

There was no sign of life.

Philippe strode into the restaurant, stopping so abruptly that Henry cannoned straight into the back of him.

Some of the dining chairs had been knocked over, and tables nearest the kitchen were skewed at every angle, their white cloths saturated and mottled with flaky grey ash.

'What is this? Where is everyone?'

'Philippe! I couldn't warn you!' Elspeth burst into the room. Her soft green blouse and skirt were stained with great damp patches. Behind her, came Arnaud and Jenna.

Philippe's relief turned to anger. 'How did this happen? And when?' He brushed past them, through the swing door and into the kitchen. There was silence. They waited. When he came back to the restaurant, he was rubbing his eyes. 'Tell me this is a nightmare!'

'There's no sign of a break-in.' Elspeth's voice cracked with the strain she was suffering. 'Someone must have hidden before we locked up last night.'

With her husband's comforting arm around her, she seemed smaller than ever. 'While we were asleep, he soaked the log basket with spirit that he'd taken from the bar. This morning, Bertrand cleaned the range and stacked it. When he struck a match, the logs exploded!' Beneath the grime, her face was ashen.

'Thank heavens, he wasn't injured!'

Jenna cast a dejected glance around the restaurant, her heart sinking even further. So much work was needed before it could be used again.

'The smoke got in here, as you see, but somehow we held back the flames. Then the fire brigade came.' She, like Elspeth, was filthy. Exhausted, too, in body and mind. She'd been happy yesterday after Luc brought her home, reliving the hours they'd spent together. 'Together' was a new concept when it came to describing their relationship. Daybreak and this latest evil had cruelly flung her back to earth.

'I thought I heard a sound in the

night.' Pushing back a strand of hair, her dirty fingers left more streaks on her cheek. 'I came to see if anything was wrong. Everywhere was quiet — restaurant, bar, kitchen, function room. The doors and windows were locked.'

Quickly she pressed her lips together as her voice quivered. After a moment, she went on. 'Whoever it was, took their time. He didn't bother to attack me. He just waited for me to go back to bed and then, so spitefully and deliberately, organised a catastrophe.'

'Not a catastrophe, my dear!' Philippe was recovering his usual sangfroid. 'Nothing more than slight inconvenience!' A good-humoured, still-handsome man of fifty, he generated a reassurance and warmth which was sheer balm. A watery smile from Jenna and a peck on the cheek from Elspeth brought his reward. 'Bertrand had a lucky escape. And so did you!'

Henri, a bird-like little man, had been tutting in the background. He left reluctantly after Philippe persuaded him there was nothing more he could do.

Arnaud was checking the stores, to see what, if anything, could be salvaged.

Bertrand started washing the kitchen ceiling. Smoke and ash had penetrated every corner of the room. He grunted instructions to Suzette. Dourly, she made a start on the walls and shelves.

Jenna couldn't help wondering. It was hard to imagine Suzette creeping around here in the night. But had she smuggled Claude into the building? There were plenty of hiding places — not least the alcove near the dresser.

There was a bigger question, and she dreaded the answer. What was the point of starting a fire? Was it a final attack, to empty the place? It seemed the unknown 'someone' was desperate to search every stone of the old inn, even if this meant burning it to the ground!

Although Elspeth was worried that Philippe would do more than was wise, she couldn't hide her relief as he took charge. He suggested that they should convert the function room into temporary dining space for their resident guests.

Madame Giraud, a neighbour, offered to cook a simple menu which could be booked in advance, and carried from her house, a few metres along the street. Estelle knew the Frenchwoman was an excellent cook, although her skills were usually reserved for her jovial and overweight husband.

The following hours were spent clearing the mess. Elspeth insisted that Philippe would be of most service if he tackled the paperwork which had accumulated during his absence. Although still suffering discomfort from his accident, he was mending rapidly. The results of his heart tests were good but she was determined that he should still take the simple precautions suggested by the doctors.

After a late lunch of bread and cheese, Jenna brought a tray of coffee to where her aunt and uncle were quietly talking. Beside them a window over-looked the river, which rippled today as though reflecting their unsettled mood. Bertrand was in the store-house. Arnaud had gone home, hands and clothing showing evidence of his efforts.

Even Suzette had worked well. Jenna could hardly believe her ears when she'd heard the girl humming under her breath. Was it a victory song that Claude had thrust one more dagger in the hopes of Philippe and Elspeth?

'This inn belonged to my father, and his father before him.' As he leant back in an armchair, Philippe reaffirmed thoughts which Elspeth had shared with Jenna these past few weeks. 'Of course they suffered setbacks and problems. It is only what one expects in business. The hotel and restaurant trade in any tourist area is bound to fluctuate according to the seasons.' Ladling two heaped teaspoons of sugar into his cup, he ignored Elspeth's protest.

'Philippe! Your heart! The doctors said . . .'

'Pah! to my heart and Pah! to the doctors. At least for today,' he amended with a mischievous glance as he read his wife's face. The colour had returned to her cheeks and, despite the shadow of anxiety at the back of her eyes, Elspeth was markedly happier.

'We must consider our options.' He and Elspeth tended to switch seamlessly from one language to the other. Despite a strong accent, his knowledge of English was excellent. The fact that today Philippe spoke in his native tongue made Jenna realise that, contrary to outward appearance, he was more seriously disturbed by today's incident than he was prepared to admit.

'For myself,' he said, 'I do not like, but I am not afraid of animosity towards the Auberge des Fleurs, or towards us personally. Although, I must say, it is like nothing my family has previously encountered.'

Jenna bit her lip. Was this the moment to tell them her suspicions?

That the root of their problem might be a legend dating from the time of Richard the Lionheart? That someone — maybe Auguste Jalabert and his son, or the Paris lawyer — wanted to drive them away? A nocturnal visitor was convinced that he'd find something of value here?

But she knew enough of their characters to realise it would only serve to harden their determination to stay. And, by staying, they would inevitably be open to more danger. As she wavered, Philippe went on talking.

'My health has become an issue — only slight, but perhaps I shall grow less active. It is Nature's way, after all.' Taking Elspeth's hand, he twisted her wedding ring around her finger. 'We have no children to continue the family tradition. It may be that the time has come to retire.'

It was late afternoon when Jenna, struggling with a huge armful of pots and pans, received a visitor. Elspeth and

Philippe were busily occupied else-where, and she was alone.

With an irritable grunt, Luc took her burden from her. 'Where do you plan to carry these?'

'The sink, please.' Already she had washed her way through a mountain of crockery and then taken it to the undamaged side of the restaurant, covering everything with clean sheets. Her smile was rueful. 'As you can see, we've had a fire. Our gremlins have been at work again.'

His narrowed eyes took in the damp, gleaming kitchen and, through the open door, the disordered restaurant. 'Have you informed the police?'

Her smile fled. Luc's stony face showed no trace of concern. Abrupt, even aggressive, his attitude was a world apart from yesterday's companionship. The green eyes which swept over her held unmistakeable dislike. What was wrong?

'Of course we've told them!' Because she had hoped for, even expected, moral support, Jenna's raw nerves snapped. Tossing cutlery into a metal pan, she heard it clatter, and enjoyed his involuntary wince. 'But first we had to cope with the fire. What else did you expect? There was no time to prance around 'phoning the gendarmerie.' Her hostility matched his. It was the only defence.

Luc's mouth tightened.

'Uncle Philippe's here. He's dealing with everything.' She pinned a neat smile across her mouth. 'It's good of you to call, but we've got everything in hand now, thanks.' It was meant as a dismissal. Later she would wonder what, within hours, had caused this inexplicable change in the man who had earlier captured her heart.

Under his breath he said something she couldn't catch. He ran one hand through his hair. Fleetingly Jenna realised that he and Guy must visit the same barber. Like his nephew, Luc's thick dark curls were cropped short. With his other hand he indicated

Bertrand's wheelbarrow which stood beside the range, laden with debris.

'I did not know about the fire. I came to tell you to leave St Justin,' he said abruptly. 'If your uncle is here and in control of the hotel, there need be no delay. Your task is done.' He took a deep breath. 'And from Madeleine's account, it is more than done.'

As Jenna's raised startled eyes, she realised he was seething with emotions which signalled nothing but trouble.

'What are you talking about?' she asked, bewildered. 'Why should I leave? After this morning's fiasco I'm needed more than ever!'

'You are mistaken! Now that your aunt has her husband's support, any young girl can do this work.' Both tone and expression were disparaging. 'Better you return to your job in a grubby newspaper office!'

'You're talking rubbish!' She didn't know which reaction came first, astonishment, hurt or outrage. Only one day earlier, as they explored Limeuil, she

121

had sensed mutual trust and liking, albeit a fresh and tiny flame. Today, Luc was stamping that delicate flame dead. Why? And why so brutally?

The answer hit hard. Of course! How could she have been such a fool? Her heart would ache, but at this hateful moment all she could feel was rage. Yesterday, the lord of the manor had descended from his pinnacle and relaxed with one of his minions, the girl from the local inn. Today he regretted it.

'I'm not leaving till I'm good and ready,' she said. Her chin lifted and her slim body straightened.

Luc's expression subtly altered. With her long, shining hair, fragile bone structure, and the challenge of silver-grey eyes, she was enticingly and utterly beautiful and his eyes could not hide his reaction.

'And what's this about Madeleine?' Forcing herself to appear composed, Jenna spread her hands in unconscious appeal, as once before, when she and

Luc had walked in harmony along the riverbank. 'I don't understand.'

'Do you pretend to know nothing of your colleagues' visit to the chateau? You told them we would be absent!' He took a step forward, his expression sardonic as Jenna retreated. 'Your plans were thwarted, were they not, when Madeleine remained home?' His teeth gleamed in the travesty of a smile. 'She proved tough opposition — unlike Madame Dupont, an elderly house-keeper, who might be beguiled with flattery and a handful of coins!'

'What happened? Is Madeleine alright?'

'Stop this farce! You know the answers. But I will tell you anyway, so there can be no mistake.' Razor-sharp eyes scrutinised Jenna's white face. 'By lunchtime, my sister-in-law felt able to leave her room. She heard footsteps in the courtyard. From the window, she saw your two buffoons, the ones who pretend such interest in geology.'

He must mean the Hargreaves brothers. They'd heard her talk of the planned outing to Limeuil and decided to take advantage while they were gone. Surely they knew they were trespassing?

'You can't blame me for that!'

As though her words lit a touch-paper, Luc ignited. Startled, she recalled her earliest impression. This wasn't the shower of icy splinters that she'd expected if Luc ever lost control. He was in the grip of white-hot fury.

'Not content with two predators, you send a third! This one had been sneaking about inside the keep. Madeleine saw him come to the library window and examine the catch, ready to force an entry.'

'Who was he? What did he want?' Jenna drew back as he came closer, looking ready to throttle her. She was prepared to defend herself — but surely he wouldn't touch her!

'You ask me who? When you already know the answer! Madeleine has visited St Justin many times and would have remembered him. His clothes and accent proclaimed him a stranger.'

'Did Madeleine ask his business?'

'Of course! He said you both work in Paris and for the same newspaper. He indicated that you are more than friends.' Condemnation tainted every word. 'You told him there was reason to believe the legend was true. You said he must search every corner, look where others had not.'

He thumped his fist so hard against the wall that Jenna actually flinched.

'You deceived us with tales of lovable insects! You befriended a lonely child! And, all the time, you and your lover planned betrayal. You thought to succeed where we have failed!'

'That's not true!'

'Would you have been content with a mere story?' Cynicism deepened the grooves beside his mouth. 'I think you would soon forget your so-called 'career' if you had found something of value!'

'What about the awful things that have happened to my family?' Jenna had almost lost her power of speech, but now she was ready to fight back. 'How do I know that you're not behind these attacks? It would suit you — more than most — to drive us out of this building!'

It was a fear that she had hidden even from herself. 'You'd buy the inn, despite your pleas of poverty. And then you'd be free to climb into the roof, pull panelling off walls, dig up floors, set the place on fire . . . again!'

'What are you saying? You think that I . . . ?' Disgust outlined his dark features. Grabbing Jenna's arms, he ignored her gasp of pain. 'Be assured, English miss, that your troubles have nothing . . . ' — he shook her — 'I tell you . . . nothing to do with me!' With a final shake, he released her.

As though physical contact had taken the centre from the storm, he said more quietly, 'If you speak the truth, it seems that there is a person who is increasingly desperate to find what, if anything, is hidden.'

'Well then, that's a problem I shall

stay here and face!' Jenna hadn't given in, and she didn't intend to.

'And if next time the victim is you, you stupid woman?' His olive skin was flushed, his glittering eyes bent on bowing her to his will.

'I'd invite you to the funeral right now. But don't bother to come!' snarled Jenna through clenched teeth.

'In that case, we will say farewell here and now.'

She should have been warned. A threatening softness had stolen into his voice. Luc tugged her towards him and lowered his mouth to hers. It was like no kiss she had ever experienced. This was hard and punishing, the culmination of deep and furious masculine frustration. But then, almost imperceptibly, his lips grew gentle, moving softly against hers until, with a harsh imprecation, he thrust her away from himself.

Turning to the sink, Jenna plunged her hands into the soapy water to hide their trembling. With head bent, and stinging eyes, she began to scour a pan furiously. All she wanted was for Luc to leave.

The slamming door told her that he had gone.

7

It was a sombre trio who ate Madame Giraud's casserole that evening. Jenna soon excused herself, feeling that her aunt and uncle would want to be alone. It was too early for bed but, in any case, she wouldn't sleep. The Auberge des Fleurs and its troubles had taken precedence over everything, even the children's book she'd been planning. Where was her precious professionalism?

Physically tiring work was a reasonable excuse. But a mind preoccupied with irrelevancies such as Luc de Villiers was no excuse at all!

This evening was a golden opportunity to put together the notes and sketches she'd already made. All it needed was will-power.

The plan didn't work at first. It seemed impossible to get started.

Sighing, she unclipped her portfolio of sketches and scattered them across the bed. In the early weeks, she had captured impressions of small animals, river views, rocky escarpments, a medley of wild flowers and grasses, but mostly her cast of characters, the insects. She considered them with critical eyes. Some of the drawings were mediocre, but one or two weren't bad — in fact, they were halfway decent. Marginally, her spirits lifted.

They rose even more as she berated herself. 'How limp can you get, Jenna Edwards?' Forget lacerated feelings — surely she could salvage something positive from being with Luc?

The first step might be to re-live, mentally, their meetings — even the painful ones. As a starting-point, what about the day when she had first met Guy?

Luc had descended like a thunder-cloud. Furtively, she'd tried to cover Albert and Oswald Ant's hideaway. Her smile flickered. The glimmer of an idea came, and with it a familiar bubble of anticipation.

Stretching across the bed, she groped inside the cabinet for her sketchpad.

The thick paper block came out and, with it, the slim volume of natural history lent by Madeleine de Villiers. There had been no chance to read it but she could glance through the pages; there might be something she could use.

Tucking a pillow behind her back, she propped herself against the bed-head and opened the leather-bound manual which had belonged to Hugo de Villiers. It was obviously very old. Entranced, she turned the fragile leaves, finding page after page of beautifully drawn insects. Some were familiar, others less so, and a few were completely unknown to her. Jenna reached the centre.

There, Hugo's marker was a folded sheet, torn from an exercise book. She could see from a series of pencil lines that he, too, had been sketching. How good an artist had he been? Curious, she spread out the paper.

Her eyes widened.

His work wasn't what she had expected. No dragonfly wings, no mottled caterpillar, no querulous ants. Instead, set into a rugged cliff, there was the outline of a building. Its chimney pointed towards the sky like some medieval giant's finger, culled from fairytales.

'The old bake-house!' She bent closer.

Hugo must have delved beneath the undergrowth where Guy had fallen. He had sketched the dry-stone retaining wall and the cottage as he imagined they'd been built, in days when the village had been prone to attack by the English, and others. At the far end of the wall, he'd outlined the crevice in the cliff-face.

A series of dotted lines beneath what were, nowadays, mostly ruins puzzled Jenna. Did he mean them to represent a footpath?

But they didn't make sense . . . unless the path led below the ground! A tremor of excitement shook her fingers as she held the paper near the light. The dots led from where Guy had been trapped and followed the natural incline of the terrain to its highest point, the unmistakeable shape of the chateau.

What did it mean? Madeleine had remarked on Hugo's excitement the night before his accident. He'd said that he hoped to find more, perhaps different, insects. Was he teasing, waiting until he was certain? His desk had been littered with old maps and plans of the chateau and St Justin.

Jenna's heart was galloping beneath her ribs. Had he been on the verge of finding something incredible, a tunnel which led from the bakery to the chateau?

Even her hands were clammy now. She recalled Madame Dupont's words as they drove to Limeuil. One of the innkeeper's daughters, Adele, had married a local man and for generations their descendants continued to bake for the villagers of St Justin.

Did she help her sister, the tragic Celestine, to meet the lord's son by means of a secret route — one which started, not from the inn, but from Adele's new home? So many questions, and so few answers!

Jenna scrambled upright. Pacing the room, hands pressed against her temples, she tried to work out the implications. Imagination brought a wealth of images to mind, moving to and fro across the years.

'Jenna, you're getting nowhere. Calm down.' The sound of her own voice made her sit again on the edge of the bed.

Starting with the smallest finger on her left hand, she ticked off possibilities. Firstly, someone was determined to get the Auberge des Fleurs by fair means or foul. Second, she was increasingly certain they had no interest in it as a business investment. Third, they believed in the legend of Marcel, and that he'd hidden something of value. Fourth and finally, she reached her index finger. Figuratively, it pointed in an unwavering line to Hugo's plan.

Everything fell into place. The answer was so obvious: if the legend was based on fact, she knew where to search. At last, Elspeth and Philippe could be rid of their tormentor. It was time to sing, dance, to swing on a star!

She glanced at her watch. Midnight. It was late but the moon was almost full tonight, the sky bright with stars. There was a fair-sized torch in the office. This was the time to look for Hugo's pathway, if only to satisfy her own curiosity. Caution warned that she might be wrong. But an inner voice whispered — no, shouted — that she was right.

Quietly, she went through the reception area. It was deserted. She turned the key and the heavy door shut behind her with a soft click. Outside, the air was fresh, laced with perfumes of the night. Shrubbery, silvered by moonlight, rustled slightly. A cat startled her as it leapt from one wall to another.

Swiftly and soundlessly, Jenna made her way to the nearest flight of steps and started climbing. The village street had seemed deserted. Even so, she hugged the shadows of the walls.

Reaching the terrace, where the ground was uneven and the drop steep, she trod carefully. All was quiet, although chimney smoke rose from some steeply-pitched rooftops below, their lighted windows strangely companionable.

Soon she came to the place where, little more than a week ago, she heard Guy's call for help. Lightly she climbed over the low parapet, dropping onto the hard surface a metre below. Crouching, she inched her way through a tunnel of brambles. At the end was a black, vertical slit, waiting.

The crevice was choked with small boulders and knotted roots. It took every ounce of strength to tear some away. At last she managed to dislodge one thick tendon. Others broke away more easily, displacing a shower of rubble. The torch showed that the fissure was deep. Was she slim enough — and brave enough — to see how far it went?

Briefly, Jenna wavered. Then she shrugged off her jumper. Twisting sideways, she tried to slide through and into the void. Impossible! But Hugo knew St Justin. And he'd believed there was a way . . .

The gap seemed to be blocked by a large, needle-shaped rock. Standing with her back against the opposite bank, she edged her feet up until the soles of her trainers pressed against the slab. Then, bracing herself, she pushed hard. Incredibly, it fell aside with a dull thud.

Even in the half-light, Jenna realised that, embedded in grit and soil, it wasn't part of the natural land mass. Someone, years ago, had deliberately forced the rock into this space. The thrill of discovery fired every nerve in her body. Her skin prickled, not with fear, but with the joy of adventure. Moonlight showed an entrance. An entrance to what?

One final wriggle and she was through. Impenetrable blackness. Experiencing a sense of space, air that was different, dampness made her reach back for her sweater. The strange, enfolding atmosphere was bringing shiver upon shiver. Tightening her grip on the torch, she directed its beam upwards, to the left and to the right, and then to a sparkling track-way. It was like a fairy grotto!

Delicate limestone formations had created an underground cathedral, where a vaulted roof reached towards the heavens. Illuminated by the pale light, it glittered as if all the stars in the universe had gathered here, a myriad of crystal stalactites. She lowered the torch. Rising from the floor of the cave, a forest of exotically shaped stalagmites surrounded her.

Instinct led her towards a recess where a series of frosted ledges imitated the steps of a great Roman temple. At the very top, just above her head, Jenna's breath caught. Time stood still.

Sheltered by a dome of shimmering aragonite was a crystal nymph. Centuries of wear from drops of water had blurred her outline but, still beautiful, she was a replica of the statue that stood on a plinth outside the chateau. There, the marble nymph looked yearningly towards the east. Here in the depths, the crystal figure seemed to smile, her arms stretched out towards . . .

'Marcel!' At last, Jenna understood. 'Of course!' Adele, knowing the lovers' secret, had told them about the hidden grotto. This was where they regularly met, the nymph their only witness. It would have made the perfect rendezvous, midway between the chateau and the inn.

After Celestine's death, Marcel must have sealed all access. In time, the secret cavern, and the ethereal figure keeping watch inside, had been forgotten.

Spellbound, following the pale yellow path of her torch, Jenna climbed the silvered steps. Reaching upwards, she touched the still form. Her own fingers were cold, but the nymph's told of frozen years in this wonderland.

Moving closer, wanting to see its face more clearly, her ankle caught on something sharp. Automatically, she bent to rub her leg. The torch beam fell across a coffer which rested at the base of the figure. The size of a small shoebox, it was made of stone and carved with intricate symbols. Kneeling on the narrow ledge, she lifted the lid, and gasped.

Inside the container was a long string of coloured stones. With trembling hands, Jenna lifted it out and, curious, rubbed it against her sweater. The jewels, dulled by their long sleep, began to glisten.

'So Marcel did bring home a

treasure! This was for Celestine.' Her whisper echoed eerily as shadows parted to reveal the story's ending. From the beginning, Jenna had felt drawn to the girl from the village inn.

Waiting for her lover's return, Celestine was destroyed by a lie. Devastated by her death, and the loss of their child, Marcel never married. The grotto had been their haven, a place of joy — and of anguish.

'The crystal figure and the necklace were his only remaining link with Celestine.' Tears pricked Jenna's eyes as she smoothed the precious stones with sensitive fingers. 'And by creating a marble image in the courtyard, he could see her every day.'

'Poetically phrased, but you guess correctly, my dear!' The voice was an electric shock, fragmenting her visions of the past.

At the foot of the steps stood Robert Selwyn and his triumphant smile. A tall man, he reached up and plucked the necklace from her hand.

'We must thank you for saving us many hours of searching.'

For seconds, Jenna was paralysed. Now she sprang to furious life.

'Do you mean that you're the toad who attacked my uncle?' she demanded. 'You're the monster who's been trying to get rid of us?'

'I'm afraid so,' he said, mockingly apologetic. Gold-rimmed spectacles reflected the scanty light and hid the expression in his pale eyes. 'Your aunt is very resilient, very stubborn. She wasted our time by refusing to leave. You, on the other hand, were most helpful in leading Fernande and me here tonight.'

He glanced over his shoulder. Until now, Jenna hadn't noticed the shadowy outline behind him. Seeing it, she realised the extent of her danger. These people had contrived long and hard. They wouldn't allow a solitary English girl to stand in their way!

'What made you so sure something was hidden?' This was no time to be afraid. The Selwyns had too much to lose. They would have to silence her — permanently. If they didn't, the law would follow them to England, or wherever they tried to hide. Keep *him talking, divert his attention*, she told herself. *Then jump and knock him off-balance.* What to do about the other man, she had no idea. But she could fight.

As he began to answer, his companion interrupted. A flashlight shone in Jenna's eyes. 'You waste time with talk! We must be quick.' He stepped forward. It was the man she had seen with the couple at the café in Lamache.

'You're going nowhere!' she exploded. Somehow she'd stop them!

Nowhere, nowhere! echoed around the multicoloured walls, the huge crystal chamber was ringing with unseen voices.

Her anger erupted. This Frenchman was an opportunistic crook. But Selwyn and his wife were disgusting! They'd ingratiated themselves with everyone, whilst at the same time inflicting misery

— dangerous misery — on the Auberge des Fleurs. Forgetting her precarious perch, Jenna grabbed at the necklace. The torch dropped and went out as she crashed down the icy steps.

Unwittingly, Robert Selwyn broke her fall. The weight of her body knocked him backwards against the man he'd called Fernande. Their flashlight hit the floor, leaving inky blackness.

'You fool!'

Jenna didn't know which man shouted. The atmosphere was punctuated by curses as they tried to untangle themselves.

This was her chance! Feverishly she felt the ground around her. The torch must be somewhere. Her fingers touched a string of small stones. The necklace! Snatching it up, her arm brushed against the lowest step. The nymph would be facing ahead, just above her. It meant that escape led towards the left.

'Hang on!' A thin light flickered. Flinging herself behind a knot of stalagmites, Jenna hugged her knees close to her chest. Both the Selwyns were smokers.

Robert had remembered the cigarette lighter he had in his pocket.

Crouched behind a twisted column, she scarcely dared to breathe. The men were swearing, one in English, and the other in French. She almost smiled. Whatever the language, those words wouldn't be in a dictionary!

The miniscule light sent a halo of rainbow colours across the glistening walls.

'Let's go, before this thing packs up.' Selwyn was starting to panic. 'Or we'll never find our way out! We'll have to come back.'

'There is no time. In any case, she will hide the jewels.'

'Then there's not one thing we can do!' The older man's voice rose a pitch.

'We cannot let her talk!' Fernande was dangerous.

'She won't talk. We'll cover the entrance so they'll never find her. We can lay a trail to the river, as if she went for a swim.'

Thanks a heap, Mr. Robert Selwyn, book-buyer extraordinaire! Jenna seethed quietly to herself.

The men and their tiny flame began to move away. Luck was taking them in the right direction. Ahead, all was black, but Jenna feared being alone in even greater blackness. A warren of tunnels and caves probably led from here, some to shallow pools or even deeper lakes. If she lost her way, there would be the final blackness . . . death. Shuddering, she rose to her feet with great care, and followed, keeping her distance.

All went well until Selwyn's light flickered and died. Violently, he swore again. Then, an exultant shout. 'Moonlight!'

It took all her willpower to stay quiet while, outside the cleft, they struggled to heave the slab to its original position. Surely they wouldn't leave her? But it would be fatal to expect mercy.

Philippe's injuries proved how ruthless they could be. They'd gone too far to retreat, and Jenna knew too much.

If they did return, her chance to escape could be when they searched for the necklace. But commonsense said they wouldn't risk coming back, knowing how little chance they stood of finding it.

Elspeth would alert everyone. Eventually, the disturbed undergrowth would be noticed — perhaps — but coldness and hunger might have done their worst by then. There was no point in wondering if Luc would be at her funeral and if he would feel any guilt.

Even here, in this dark chamber, a hand clenched her heart as Jenna remembered their final encounter. Miserably she wondered if she had imagined his earlier warmth, the tenderness of his kiss. Even if Simone was his first and final choice, Jenna had no doubt that he'd liked, and been attracted by, the girl from the inn who dared to defy his medieval and lordly ways.

The slab was back in place. All was quiet. Robert Selwyn would hurry to the Auberge des Fleurs. His wife and Fernande were bound to agree that return could be futile. Automatically Jenna's fingers touched the string of precious stones beneath her sweater. Rachel wouldn't take defeat well. Thwarted greed was an uncomfortable bedfellow.

They would rely on Jenna being found too late, if at all. Selwyn would leave a note, she guessed, to be found next morning. It would profoundly regret that urgent business recalled him to England, but say that he and his wife hoped to return soon. By leaving money to settle their bill, he would give Elspeth and Philippe no reason to connect the couple with their niece's disappearance. The Selwyns would be safe, but at least they'd go empty-handed.

Inside the grotto, Jenna could see nothing, but she knew that, by progressing in a straight line, she should reach the blocked entrance.

Until now, the darkness had been a friend. But now, out of that darkness came a muffled whir, a stirring of the air as it came alive. Black shapes swooped close. Bats! Jenna ducked her head with a cry of revulsion. She was terrified of bats! It was an irrational fear, but very real.

She ran. The uneven floor caught her foot, and brought her down. Her head struck an outcrop of rock and she crumpled, senseless and unconscious.

8

A blinding headache was the first sensation. Jenna's eyes opened. Why did she feel so cold? The damp, enveloping atmosphere of the great cavern brought memory flooding back. Painfully she stood, hoping for a glimmer of light. There was none. Sinking back down to the floor, she waited for a spasm of nausea to pass. Her temple was throbbing. Touching it gently, she winced.

Of course, she'd fallen. And bats — an army of bats! She scrambled to her feet and fought rising panic. Everywhere was dark. Crouching, she ran both hands across the flat bedrock. Was this a track, the one leading into the grotto? Where had her wild flight ended?

'I can't have run far.' Her voice broke the uneasy hush, but not the nightmare.

Inching forward, she splayed her fingers across the ground. Incredibly, they met a familiar shape. Luck, or blind instinct, had again led her to the recess where she'd seen the pyramid of ledges. Above her, unseen, was the nymph.

Stretching upwards, Jenna touched a frost-glazed limb, knowing that she had found a friend who, silently reassuring, pointed towards the outside world.

She crawled along the uncertain path, terrified of losing it, or slipping into some bottomless crevice. At last, ahead, came a chink of light and, silhouetted, the big rock. Sobbing uncontrollably, she leant her cheek against its hard contours. Soon she would be walking along the terrace, down the steps and into the Auberge des Fleurs.

But, despite every desperate effort, the rock wouldn't budge. Finally, she slumped, exhausted.

'I'll do better once my head stops thumping,' she told herself. She must not allow herself to have any negative thoughts. Settling on the floor, her back propped against the rock, Jenna slept.

A long time later, she awoke, stiff and chilled. Wrapping both arms around her body, she wriggled her fingers and toes, trying to bring them back to life.

An empty stomach didn't help: she'd hardly eaten yesterday because of the upset of the fire. Slivers of daylight around the blocked entrance mocked her. Safety was within reach. So near — and yet, still so far!

Only minutes away, Elspeth would be frantic. She and Philippe would fear the worst, suspecting the work of their unknown enemy. Robert and Rachel Selwyn would have gone, leaving no reason for anyone to connect their departure with Jenna's disappearance.

Hours passed. The slab wouldn't budge. Once, she heard voices on the terrace. She shouted until she was hoarse, her cries swallowed up within the cave. Daylight began to fade. Shivering and hungry, she drifted once again into an uneasy sleep.

* * *

When the rock was dragged from the entrance, she didn't wake. Nor did she hear Luc's exclamation as flashlights played across her huddled figure. Raw cold and the dank atmosphere had penetrated every bone.

Momentarily, her eyes opened as strong arms lifted her. Later, there was a hazy memory of a man who must have been a doctor, and Elspeth's gasp as she found Celestine's necklace underneath Jenna's damp sweater.

Urgently, she caught her aunt's hand. Elspeth bent close.

'Rest now, my love. You're safe!'

'The Selwyns! Stop them!' It was a whisper but the message was clear.

Instantly, Elspeth understood. Her look was so savage that Jenna smiled weakly before drifting back to sleep.

It was almost lunchtime next day before they talked properly. Elspeth insisted that Jenna should stay in bed until the doctor was satisfied with her condition. A longer confinement underground could have led to fatal hypothermia.

She said that Robert and Rachel Selwyn had driven to the airport, hoping for an immediate flight. Bad weather conditions in England, however, delayed takeoff, so police had been waiting when they eventually landed.

Dismayed that Jenna had been found so quickly, the couple hadn't hesitated to implicate Fernande.

'The man was already known to the authorities,' said Elspeth. 'They'd traced him to Lamache, where you saw him with the Selwyns. Apparently he'd paid two local crooks to force a landslide whilst Philippe was underneath, on our patio.'

'I wonder how the Selwyns got mixed up with him?' There were still grey shadows under Jenna's eyes.

Elspeth shrugged. 'Perhaps they met here in France last year. Hot on the treasure trail, they needed help from someone with local knowledge and no scruples. They were convinced this building held the key to the mystery, and were desperate to get us out.'

'But how did they know about Marcel and the jewels?' Celestine's necklace was locked in Philippe's safe and he'd said that Jenna should be the one to hand it to Luc. The thought pleased her. Luc's accusations had been brutal. It was hard to forget her pain, and resentment too, that he couldn't bring himself to trust her. Her frozen hours in the grotto would be almost worthwhile, if they made him eat his words!

'They must have come across the legend in one of their old books,' said Elspeth. 'We'll know more when Luc has talked to the police.'

Jenna's heart leapt at the mention of his name. It seemed that he had played a significant role in her rescue, insisting that the search should concentrate on the ruined buildings, and not the river. Leading the hunt, he had 'fought like a madman', according to Bertrand, to uncover the blocked entrance.

Elspeth went to the bedroom door. 'I'll leave you to have a shower. I'll be close at hand, so shout if you feel shaky.' Mischief edged her smile. 'You need to be in good condition before you fall out with Luc again!'

She ducked as Jenna pretended to throw a slipper. Elspeth was discreet, but must have watched progress since that first stormy meeting. As for the final, dreadful, confrontation — doubtless everyone knew of Luc's brief, angry visit.

It was late afternoon before he came to the Auberge des Fleurs. Jenna had anticipated his arrival with mixed feelings.

'What a cocktail!' Absentmindedly, she traced an outline in some spilt talcum powder. 'Love, hurt, pleasure, despair — how can one man make me feel so miserable? And, on top of everything, I must thank him for rescuing me!'

With an irritable flourish, she swept her hand across the white dust, scattering it in a fine mist through the air.

Bathed, her hair shining, she wore a slim-skirted dress in dark blue linen and, when Luc arrived, was carrying out light tasks in the kitchen. He stood, hands on hips, making his exasperation clear.

Jenna waited. He'd accused her of being in league with the Hargreave brothers and, far worse, with Fernande. Would he apologise?

First, he enquired politely about her health and then suggested that she might care for a short walk.

'Unless you prefer to rest, of course.'

Jenna wasn't fooled. He was adept at getting his way. His comment was only mildly sardonic as he removed a saucepan from her hands.

'I feel fine, thank you.'

He grunted, highly suspicious of her sudden meek capitulation.

Once again, she found herself walking with him beside the river.

'There's so much to ask, that I don't know where to begin.' A rather uncertain glance betrayed the fact that she hadn't forgotten about their final head-on collision.

His rare smile appeared. 'I might say exactly the same. Perhaps we should toss a coin, to see who goes first.'

He couldn't have forgotten either. Maybe he was tacitly calling a truce.

'Well,' said Jenna. 'The most important thing is that I should thank you for finding me before I died of hypothermia.' Shuddering, she recalled icy tentacles which crept insidiously across her limbs.

'When I returned to the chateau that evening, Madeleine said your aunt had telephoned, to ask if you were there. She and your uncle were deeply worried. Your bed had not been slept in, and you could not be found. The gendarmerie found your towel and shoes on the riverbank.'

Presumably the Selwyns had taken them from Jenna's room and laid a false trail to the river. Then, in the early hours of morning, they wrote a note for Elspeth, and sped quietly away from St Justin.

'I heard the men plan my supposed drowning.' Jenna still found it difficult to talk about what had happened. 'I could only hope someone found me before I froze to death.'

'I was not convinced that you had gone to the river.' Luc contemplated the fast-flowing waters. 'Your aunt also believed you too sensible to swim alone while everyone slept. I went to your room to find evidence, either that you had left willingly, or been taken. I found Hugo's book, with the map he had made.' He looked amused by his own reaction. 'I could have jumped for joy. I knew immediately where to look for you.'

'Because of that insatiable curiosity you accuse me of?' dared Jenna. He didn't reply but the creases in his cheeks deepened. 'I saw Hugo's drawing, and everything became clear,' she said. 'My aunt and uncle were being harassed, presumably by someone determined to buy the hotel. It wasn't until I realised they were hunting for something that I wondered if the legend really had substance after all.'

She fell silent, reluctant to remind Luc how he'd snubbed her, when it was obvious that he, Madeleine and Simone believed the story to be true.

'Robert Selwyn must have arranged to meet Fernande that night. They saw me head for the terrace, and followed.'

Luc's expression was grim. 'They had no conscience about leaving you to a miserable death. Valuable time was lost in scouring the river banks.'

'I was scared of what they'd do if they caught me. That's why I hid.' Shaking off the memory, Jenna changed the subject. 'Have you discovered why the Hargreave brothers came to the chateau while we were at Limeuil?'

'Enthusiasm, opportunism and curiosity. They gave Madeleine the name of their university in England, so I checked and found them to be genuine.'

'They probably thought a sneaky look from the battlements would be easier than the rigmarole of gaining permission,' suggested Jenna. 'As for Fernande, the Selwyns' time in the library was very restricted, under Madame Dupont's sharp eyes. They needed him to spend time there.'

Her colour deepened as she looked up and met the unusual intensity of his green eyes. Quickly she bent, finding a pebble to skim across the waters. 'It seems to me they were clutching at straws. If the de Villiers family had drawn a blank — what chance had a trio of villains?'

'Whatever book led them to the legend in the first place may have also suggested Marcel's hiding place.'

'That would give them a sneaky advantage.' Jenna was still recovering from that moment of awareness. There seemed to be another conversation taking place, one which was unspoken.

'I wonder if that's why Madeleine saw Fernande coming from the keep?'

'As his close associate in a Paris newspaper office, you should know already.' Jenna cast him a dubious look. Relieved, she saw the corner of his mouth lift in a sardonic smile.

'Sorry to disillusion you,' she retorted. 'But he's really not my type!'

His face grew serious. 'I wonder exactly what is your type.'

Disconcerted, she lowered her head, to hide her expression. The only man who appealed to her was Luc himself.

Hurriedly she reminded him, 'So why d'you think Fernande was in the keep?'

Luc didn't pursue his previous question. 'The tower is empty except for narrow steps which once allowed defenders to sight potential enemies. Fernande's interest made me look more closely. I found a crowbar hidden under a sack. No doubt he meant to return there, if his search in the library proved a failure. This morning we raised the stone floor of the keep and found — '

'That it led down to the grotto!' Jenna's grey eyes shone. Clasping her hands together, she skipped like a child.

Luc laughed out loud, enjoying her excitement. 'Correct!'

'So this is how Marcel left the chateau for his secret meetings with Celestine.'

'And she, in turn, entered from the cleft beside her sister's home. It had originally been an escape route in case the chateau was besieged, its existence eventually forgotten.'

They had covered some distance by now. Luc took hold of Jenna's arm. The warmth of his fingers sent even greater heat along her veins and into her heart. Control fled whenever he touched her, but somehow she must break his spell!

'You have walked far enough. Shall we return and persuade your aunt and uncle to drink coffee with us?' He turned Jenna back the way they had come.

Luc had made no mention of the necklace. The prospect of giving it to him quickened her footsteps. Surprised, he adjusted his longer strides to hers.

At the Auberge des Fleurs, Elspeth welcomed them.

'We'll have coffee in the lounge,' she suggested. 'Everyone's out, so we can talk comfortably.'

Jenna whispered in Philippe's ear. He left the room, returning minutes later with a small package.

When she handed it to Luc, his brows contracted in surprise. As the wrappings fell away, his face changed. Speechless, he touched the necklace and then, jumping to his feet, took it to the window. Even from where she sat, Jenna could see the gems become more distinct as the sun's rays fired each colour to brilliance.

'This was with the nymph?' Luc's voice had dropped to a stunned whisper.

She nodded. 'Yes. I grabbed it from Robert Selwyn and ran.'

Lines of wonder and unbelief had erased every trace of the underlying worry which rarely left his lean features. As he held the necklace to the light, Jenna for the first time could appreciate it in daylight. Fashioned from a variety of precious stones, each was of equal size, and mounted on an intricately worked gold chain. Once expertly restored, it would be magnificent.

She stood to look more closely but, on reaching Luc, she suddenly swayed, her face chalk-white.

'You are ill!' He gripped Jenna's arms.

'No,' she faltered, furious with herself for her own weakness. 'It's just excitement. Truly, I'm fine.'

'I need my staff in good working order!' Philippe tucked her hand in his arm and, ignoring her mumbled protests, ushered Jenna to her bedroom. 'We will talk again tomorrow.'

Tomorrow seemed a long wait, but Jenna knew he was right. She slept dreamlessly and, when morning came, knew that she was back to normal.

Her spirits sank to zero, however,

when Elspeth relayed a message.

'Luc hoped to join us for lunch but sends his apologies. It's been impossible to keep discovery of the grotto quiet, so St Justin is swamped with reporters. The entrance must be secured and the area around it made safe. Once he's organised all that, he plans to take the necklace to Paris for expert examination. It's likely to be of immense historical interest, of course. And he must have discussions with umpteen different authorities.' Elspeth scanned Jenna's expressionless face. 'He insists that you are to rest properly and not talk to anyone, apart from the police.'

'Nice of him to ring,' commented Jenna tonelessly. 'Especially when he's obviously so busy.'

Elspeth held her tongue, but her eyes were dancing.

★   ★   ★

Conscious of her ordeal, the local gendarmes had already interviewed

Jenna briefly. Today, however, they returned with a senior inspector who wanted a more detailed account of events. To their file on Philippe's accident, they added other incidents for which the Selwyns or Fernande might be held responsible, including the ransack of Jenna's room and the outhouse. The fire in the kitchen was undoubtedly also their doing.

Robert Selwyn's accident had been carefully staged, with the assistance of his wife. Hidden in the alcove, she had pushed the dresser shelves off-balance. As she ran from the room, her husband dropped quickly onto the broken glass and pool of wine. No one had guessed that his unnatural pallor was just that — artificially produced with make-up.

'They switched off the ice-making machine and cancelled Elspeth's order for the council dinner,' Jenna said thoughtfully. 'But what about the cancelled bookings — how could they fix that?'

Philippe thought he'd found the

answer. 'I checked the letters which came, reserving accommodation. Once you know what you are looking for, it is easy to see that some were posted from towns in England, and even France or Germany, where the Selwyns might have attended book fairs. They used different notepaper and addresses. Bookings through the internet we accepted without question and maximum disruption was caused through cancellations.'

'They went to a lot of trouble,' said Jenna. 'Why bother?'

'Do not forget they were playing for high stakes. It was important to work slowly, try and ease us out. You must admit, neither Robert nor Rachel Selwyn appear the type to use physical harm. They grew impatient and that is when Fernande used his heavy boots on us!'

Everyone protected Jenna from media attention during the next few days, but time weighed heavily as a consequence of being confined indoors.

'As they say, today's news is tomorrow's fish and chip paper,' Elspeth assured her cheerfully. 'Interest will soon move to something else.'

The week passed without news from the chateau, although Madeleine came with flowers for Jenna.

As they sat with coffee, she revealed that Simone had returned to Paris. 'She went with Luc, but sends you her warmest greetings. She is longing to hear a minute by minute account of your adventure. She admired Celestine's necklace, of course, but says the girl would have needed a plain, preferably black, dress in order to achieve the maximum effect.'

Even as they laughed, Jenna felt a stab of familiar pain. Of course the young Frenchwoman would have accompanied Luc — why should she stay in St Justin without him? The intimate warmth of his car would enfold them as they drove to the capital. They would discuss people and places they knew, recent events, and discussions with Madeleine on how to protect Guy's inheritance, now there had been a radical change in the fortunes of his estate.

With Simone beside him, Luc would talk about the wonderful cave, but spare little thought for the girl who almost lost her life there.

9

The first indication of Luc's return came when Philippe received a telephone call inviting him, Elspeth and Jenna to dinner at the chateau. The restaurant was operational again after the disruption of the fire, so they would meet one evening when it was closed.

Jenna wanted to go; but she didn't want to go. She wished she had a new dress; but she was glad to wear the same as before. Luc would realise she had made no special effort. Emotions clouded her mind and her heart. Soon it would be time to leave St Justin . . . and to leave behind every memory of him.

Philippe casually mentioned that Simone had returned from Paris with Luc and that it would be a special celebration evening. A celebration of what? Were the couple about to announce their engagement? If they did, she would have to plaster a smile on her face, and join the congratulations.

Perhaps it would be a celebration that the grotto had been found. Elspeth and Philippe thought its discovery might bring an end to the de Villiers family's financial difficulties at long last.

'I imagine that Luc and Madeleine will consider opening it as a tourist attraction,' said Philippe. 'As for the jewels — they must be worth a fortune!'

'I can't bear to think of Celestine's necklace being sold.' Jenna's soft and wistful whisper went unheard.

The mystery of Suzette's good humour after the kitchen fire was explained by Madame Boulet. The widow called to thank Elspeth for employing her daughter but said that the girl intended to leave the village at the end of this month.

'The pauvre petite knows how you will miss her, but she has been offered a magnificent opportunity by Monsieur Jalabert.'

'Claude?' Elspeth was astounded.

The woman shook her head. 'No, no! It is Auguste, the father. He plans to send her to his friend who works in a splendid hotel in Nice. The friend will school Suzette, so that she can work in the finest establishments in France!'

Jenna was working in the background as they talked. She exchanged glances with Elspeth. Mentally, she saluted Auguste Jalabert. The Scottish phrase, 'a canny fellow' sprang to mind. It seemed that he'd become aware of Claude's interest — whether temporary or long-lasting — in Suzette and, by offering such an incentive, would stop her regular contact with his son. He might even hint that, once fully trained, she could prove an asset to an ambitious young hotelier. A wily fellow indeed!

Suzette's mother was struggling to express her regret. 'At the beginning of the tourist season and you will be without a waitress!'

Jenna buried her face in a vase of yellow tulips as she heard her aunt reassure the little woman. 'Don't upset yourself, Madame Boulet. There are sure to be young girls wanting summer work. We shall manage — although,' Elspeth had to steady her voice, 'Suzette will be a great loss!'

Ushering her visitor to the door, she scowled horribly at Jenna, who had collapsed into silent giggles. Returning a few minutes later, Elspeth, too, laughed until the tears ran down her face.

★　★　★

But laughter didn't come easily as Jenna waited for the evening when she would see Luc again.

As she arrived at the chateau with her aunt and uncle, the lights were blazing and a smiling Madeleine waited to greet them at the open door. She led them through the great stone-walled hall. As ever, Guy's mother was elegantly clad, her short deep purple evening dress ornamented only by silver loops in her ears.

In the lounge, Jenna's gaze immediately flew to Luc, devastatingly handsome in a black evening suit. Greeting Elspeth with his attractive smile, he raised her hand to his lips in a gesture which seemed entirely natural in these medieval surroundings. Her colour rose, but she responded graciously.

As he came forward to welcome Jenna, she was prepared, and able to accept the touch of his lips on the back of her hand with a formal smile. His eyes held slight surprise, although he merely said, 'You are looking better. But you still appear rather pale.' For seconds longer, he assessed her in what she could only describe as an avuncular manner.

As a compliment his comment was a non-runner she decided, and muttered a non-committal reply. It seemed that, as her rescuer, Luc had assumed the right to tell her she looked washed-out! Smoothing cold hands down the sides of her skirt, a quick glance reassured her. There was no need to creep into the shadows. Although Luc had seen the grey silk dress before, she knew how it flattered her slender fairness.

His mouth slanted in self-mockery, noting her relief when Guy entered the room. Seeing Jenna, the boy whooped with pleasure and gave her such an ecstatic hug that all formality vanished.

As for the promised celebration — Simone had followed closely behind him. With her came a tall, slim man. His light brown hair had been trimmed by an expert, his evening wear the product of expensive tailoring, but his thin face with its aquiline nose was intelligent and good-natured.

'My darling Alain couldn't resist being one of the first to visit Jenna's wonderful discovery,' announced Simone, a vision of sophistication in her favourite black. On this occasion, her sleek lace dress had a daringly low neckline which revealed self-assurance as well as creamy skin. 'We have decided to drink champagne all evening because nothing less will do!'

Luc drew her companion forward.

'May I more formally,' with a meaningful glance at Simone, who pulled a face at him, 'introduce my friend and partner, Alain Courbet. As a superb architect he has carried the weight of our business during my recent absences. And as a friend he is beyond price.'

Jenna realised that she had been mistaken when she accompanied Simone to Limeuil. There, Madeleine's sister had unwittingly led her to assume that Alain was her employer.

She was still readjusting her ideas when Simone, with a friendly embrace, brushed a perfumed cheek against her own.

'I learnt how you found Marcel's cave, but have many questions!' A slight crease marred the perfection of her forehead as, unashamedly, she scrutinised Jenna. 'But I see traces of the strain you suffered. You knew terror, as well as wonder,' she said sympathetically. 'If you prefer to forget, I shall try to be content with tales of your insect friends.' Luc's sweetheart had great charm, even if she was about to break Jenna's heart.

Philippe placed his arm around Jenna's slight shoulders and squeezed them gently. Was he aware of her tension, she wondered gratefully? His quiet strength and reassurance made Jenna realise yet again how fortunate Estelle had been in her choice of husband.

To Guy's disgust, Madeleine insisted that he must be content with lemonade, whilst the adults accepted sparkling crystal glasses from Luc. His duties as host completed, he joined Philippe and Elspeth who, relieved of the storm clouds which had hung over them, were in a festive mood.

Jenna felt his eyes following her as she tried to drift unobtrusively to the far side of the room, where Guy was impatiently waiting. There was undeniable solace in the fact that the child regarded her as his personal property.

Dinner was a lively affair, but Jenna had little appetite. Seated at Luc's right hand, she knew he noticed her near-silence, although conversation flowed across the table at a rate which made it unnoticeable to the others.

Shaking her head when he offered to prepare a peach, she thanked him for moving her plate aside. Polite but impenetrable reserve was her only protection. He didn't attempt to provoke or even tease her — she must be looking particularly fragile. If he was intent on taking care of her tonight, it must be gratitude that she had helped to secure Guy's future.

Alain was an engaging, cultured man, who had known the de Villiers family for years. Sitting next to Simone, with Elspeth opposite him, he amused them with anecdotes about a client whose quirky demands upset each stage of the building process. In turn, Simone entertained them with bizarre incidents from her world of haute couture.

Conversation inevitably turned to the grotto.

'Have you managed to discover yet what it was that first set Robert Selwyn so confidently on to the trail of the treasure?' Elspeth asked Luc.

'Yes, the police learnt a good deal through their questions,' he said easily. 'As you know, Selwyn and his wife trade in antiquarian books. A year ago, they chanced upon an extremely rare biography of Richard Coeur de Lion, written soon after the Third Crusade.

'When the Crusade failed in its original quest, Richard set sail for home. He was shipwrecked on the Dalmatian coast and then, disguised as a pilgrim, captured by Leopold of Austria. A disastrous end to the project.'

Elspeth leant forward, intrigued. 'Why wasn't Marcel also captured?'

'He and other Crusaders must have returned on different ships and avoided trouble. The chronicler wrote that they brought back articles of great value.' Luc lifted his shoulders in a slight shrug. 'There was no indication then, or in later years, that the lord of St Justin had acquired money, so it was assumed that Marcel hid his share, or that the chronicler was mistaken.'

He looked around his rapt audience. 'The manuscript which came into the Selwyns' possession hinted that 'a magnificent secret' rested beneath the buildings of the village. Doubtless this referred to the grotto and its crystal nymph, but the Selwyns were focussed on valuables which could be quietly sold to a private collector.

'Marcel, they reasoned, brought home a gift for Celestine, only to discover that she was dead. If treasure did exist, it was likely to be hidden in her father's inn, because chateau owners through-out the years had found nothing. The tragedy of the romance and the fact that Marcel never married added weight to the legend, of course.'

The centuries-old tale affected everyone seated around the long candlelit table. Conversation slowed briefly until Madame Dupont brought coffee, her pleasure evident when they praised the dinner she had provided. Afterwards, Luc rose to his feet.

'We have two very special reasons for celebration tonight. Which shall we drink to first?' he asked teasingly.

Simone lifted her glass with an extravagant sweep of her hand. 'There is no competition, cheri. The de Villiers family owes much to the brave young woman who proved the legend true. Let us drink to Jenna!'

Jenna's cheeks burned beneath a chorus of congratulations. All she had done was to follow Hugo's lead and her own curiosity! Still, if she fell apart after the next toast, her tears would, with any luck, be seen as reaction to her ordeal.

The second announcement was about to come. Luc was still on his feet. He turned to Simone. Jenna forced her lips to tilt upwards. Had they really turned to stone? This was it! How could she bear to listen?

Luc's mouth was moving but she didn't hear what he said. Then Philippe and Elspeth were exclaiming, and so was Guy, who had been allowed to stay up late on this special occasion. Simone had thrown her arms around — Alain!

'We wish Simone and Alain great happiness in their marriage. Alain will need our ongoing good wishes and support, and plentiful vitamins in order to cope with his wife. But she will bring him laughter and joy — that we can guarantee!'

The remainder of the evening passed in a haze. Somehow Jenna managed to act normally, although she guessed that Elspeth's shrewd eyes easily saw beneath her flimsy façade.

It was late when Luc and Madeleine accompanied their guests to the court-yard. As he held the rear door of Philippe's car open for Jenna, Luc bent his head. For one insane moment, she thought he was about to kiss her.

Instead he murmured, 'I will see you tomorrow. I need your advice concerning the grotto and,' he hesitated, 'some other matters.'

Startled, she looked fully into his face, something she had avoided for the past few hours. In the dim light she could see only the outline of his jaw and the jut of his nose.

'But surely . . . '

A gleam of white told her he was smiling. 'Always you argue!' Placing his finger on her lips, he said, 'Hush now! Sleep well, my prickly dove.'

As so often, he had the final word because Philippe had started the engine. It was time to go.

10

It wasn't dark any more. Outside the sky was blue but here, deep in the cliff-face, limestone glistened as though it had captured an arc of shooting stars. Lanterns were strung here and there — only a few, but enough to bring the huge cavern to magical life. Jenna hadn't known how she would react to being inside the grotto again. Luc was holding her hand firmly in his. When she realised it, she wriggled her fingers, trying to break free. He wouldn't release her.

'I prefer to keep a tight grip on you,' he warned. 'You might disappear down some crevice or knock yourself unconscious again.' Only half in jest, he promised, 'I will try to protect you from any inquisitive bats.'

Dim lighting, the enclosed space, and the knowledge that they were alone, made the atmosphere disconcertingly intimate. Jenna tried to sound matter-of-fact. 'I know they won't really get tangled in my hair — I should give them more credit! It's just that they move so swiftly, I can't be sure they'll make a detour.'

He didn't hide his amusement but was sympathetic. 'I admit that I am not fond of them either — and my hair is far shorter than yours!'

He was watching Jenna closely. She realised that he, too, wondered how she would respond to being inside this underground hideaway once more. Running his free hand over her braided hair, he asked 'Are bats the reason for today's severe style?'

It was true that she had rejected her usual ponytail, but not because of the bats. Initially, for today's meeting with Luc she had decided to dress formally. A last-minute change of mind had made her scramble into cut-off jeans and hooded sweat-shirt. Why try to impress him?

'You said you wanted my advice about the grotto?' Determined to keep mental, if not physical, distance, she sounded coolly helpful. This seemed to be the safest procedure. Even to relax her guard for a moment might make Luc think she would welcome his friendship — something he would toss into a bin when it suited him.

He'd done it before. There was no guarantee that he wouldn't do it again!

'I would appreciate your opinion,' he agreed. 'Essentially, although others will come to this place and marvel at it, I hope we can preserve its very special aura . . . that of a lovers' haven.' Although he spoke quietly, still the echo came back to them in his alluringly attractive accent, *haven . . . haven . . .*

Hearing it, he smiled a little. 'You understand Celestine. You are of similar age and appearance and can relate to her lifestyle, her hopes and dreams. And you can best imagine how she felt about Marcel — his life, his love, and the rumour of his marriage.'

Although on occasion she had experienced Luc's sensitivity, Jenna had not expected him to be so in tune with her own feelings. Uneasily, she wondered how strong her defences would prove, especially as he went on speaking.

'Today everyone can see three different images of her — one fashioned from the elements, another carved from marble, the third a warm and caring, vibrant girl. In the courtyard, when I saw you with the statue, I was shaken by the physical likeness you shared. It was clear that you felt great empathy with her.'

Walking slowly, stopping to look, and listen, the silence which hung from the lofty arena was almost tangible. They reached the recess. A lantern had been cunningly placed to illuminate the crystal nymph from behind, so that her diaphanous draperies shimmered in an other-worldy way, and her shadow was projected onto the shining walls.

'She's exquisite,' whispered Jenna.

Slipping from Luc's hold, she mounted the steps and smoothed gentle fingers along the nymph's outstretched arm. The elements and time had blurred her facial expression, but the delicate body was poised as if ready to fly, and her presence was disturbingly real.

Luc's gaze locked on the two figures; Jenna touched with silver, full of life, the other girl luminous and still, but almost a mirror-image. His voice was husky. 'You will make fun of me if I say how very beautiful I find you both.'

Carefully Jenna came down the steps and, knowing she mustn't let herself be beguiled, with equal care chose her words.

'My aunt and uncle suggested that you might decide to finance the estate by opening this grotto to the public.'

'Yes.' Luc passed a hand across his eyes, as though he needed to break a spell. 'Madeleine and I agree that it is the only way to safeguard Guy's inheritance. Security will be paramount, and I have employed structural engineers to stabilize the entire area, inside and out. We must also decide whether to construct a visitors' reception through the keep, or to rebuild the bake-house, and allow access from there.'

'Entrance from the keep would enable tourists to enjoy views across the river, but it could ruin your privacy.' It was a thorny subject on which she and Luc had crossed swords the first time they met. Would he remember?

'You are right. But I must face facts. Maintenance of the chateau estate is costly. As a local landlord, it has been forced to neglect property renovations, boundaries and pastureland. Economically it has reached its lowest point. Thanks to you, we now have an alternative to enforced sale or slow decay. Madeleine and I are based in Paris because of our work, so we would only notice visitors during our holidays here.' He looked amused. 'She and Guy are excited about the possibilities. They have even talked of converting the main hall to a museum.'

'That would be fascinating!' Jenna's artistic imagination pictured how it might be achieved. 'As well as the historic interest of the building, you could, for instance, create a picture gallery, telling the story of the Crusades.'

Tentatively, she posed the question to which she feared the answer. 'Celestine's necklace — it has to be sold?'

Luc shook his head.

'Definitely not. Somehow we will find other ways of raising funds. Our plans might interest the civic authorities because the village and local area should benefit considerably from a new tourist centre.

'As for the necklace, it is being examined by experts. They are excited by its history and design. Later, it will be stored in a bank until Guy comes of age. He can then decide.' He added whimsically, 'I doubt that he will ever part with such an emotive family relic.'

'I assume that the museum would tell the legend of Marcel and Celestine.

Would it be possible to exhibit a replica of the necklace?' Jenna touched the ledge where she had found the stone casket and its breathtaking contents.

'Assuredly. I believe Celestine would be happy for the world to see Marcel's gift at long last.'

'And the genuine necklace would be safe from the likes of Rachel and Robert Selwyn — or their pal, Fernande,' added Jenna.

Fernande's role in causing Philippe's injury was without doubt, and Robert Selwyn had admitted to the kitchen fire. His wife was implicated in all that had taken place, including the lethal implications of sealing Jenna inside the grotto.

Jenna would be required to give evidence, as would Elspeth and Philippe. They didn't relish the prospect, but it was unavoidable.

Luc drew her closer, as though he had followed the course of her thoughts. 'I shall be there at the court with you. You need not be nervous.' Reflectively, he added, 'Their last thought was to benefit others but, without them, the grotto and its treasure might have remained a mystery.'

Jenna looked up at the figure, high on its frosty plinth. Unexpectedly, tears filled her eyes.

'Do you think Marcel would approve of your plans?'

'I truly believe so. Although this was the special, secret place he shared with Celestine, he would understand our need to secure his struggling estates.'

They fell silent, although an under-current of awareness made it seem as though they were still talking. Then, Luc raised Jenna's chin with gentle fingers. In the shadows her eyes were dark and wide. She felt his breath stir the fine-spun hair around her temples as she inhaled the masculine scent of his body.

'We have discussed the grotto and the necklace, and you have given your approval.' He hesitated, as though unsure of how to continue.

'You said you wanted my advice on some other things,' she ventured, her fortitude and her good intentions wavering.

His fingers tightened. 'They are all matters on which you need to agree,' he murmured. 'Can you answer 'yes' when I ask if you are content for me to hold you like this?'

With the tiniest gasp of exhilaration, she whispered in reply, 'Yes.'

'And like this?' His arms slid around her back and he drew her fully into his embrace. As though the touch of her body broke his control, a twist of urgency threaded his words. 'I have only known you for a short time, but I cannot remember a moment when I did not want to hold you so . . . and kiss you . . . like this.' His lips were firm and warm and hard on hers. They lingered, before moving to trace a feather-light path across her closed eyelids, her nose and the soft curves of her throat.

When he finally raised his head, Jenna dared to open her eyes.

'I can recall a few occasions when you didn't even like me!' she teased, safe in the knowledge that he had felt her response.

'I was aware of you from the moment we met, even though I was angry and suspicious. I told you how we had been harassed after my father and Hugo died. Your new friendship with Guy could so easily have been a ploy! How was I to know you were as innocent as you appeared?' He brushed his lips across the silky hair which his fingers had loosened until it fell freely around her shoulders. 'I dared not trust you. I was furious with myself that all I wanted was your touch, your liking, and most of all, to know you better.'

'I thought you and Simone . . . '

'The saints protect me! I am fond of Simone — who would not be? But she would drive me to insanity.' His voice dropped. 'With you, I lose my mind in a very different way!'

Shifting, he leant against one of the tall limestone columns which rose towards the dome, and tugged Jenna to rest against him. 'I hurt you by refusing to admit my belief that treasure might, in truth, be hidden. I could see the natural way in which you related to Celestine, and, hearing of events at the Auberge des Fleurs, was fearful for your safety. There were too many to be accidental but, without proof, there was little I could do to protect you.'

'I thought any concern reflected what you saw as feudal obligation towards a minion,' she challenged.

He gave a shout of laughter. 'How can you say such a thing? You matched me in every possible way with your waspish tongue and your determination not to be beaten.'

He felt her smile against his chest. 'You can be extremely lordly.'

'I apologise. You must blame my genes and not the hard-working architect that I am.' He nipped her ear gently. 'I enjoyed sparring with you — you are a worthy opponent. But increasingly I wanted your warmth, and not your hostility. I was even jealous of my own nephew!'

'And of Fernande! You accused me of being in league with him.'

'At Limeuil I felt that you and I were moving towards something special, but I did not know your feelings,' he said. 'I have never experienced such uncertainty and it unnerved me. When Madeleine told me about her unwanted visitors, I was almost relieved to decide that you had betrayed us.'

'And, instead, I was about to be entombed on your behalf,' Jenna lifted a hand to touch the crisp black curls. Catching hold, he carried it to his lips before placing a kiss in the centre of her palm. A tremor tightened his clasp until she could scarcely breathe.

'Don't even joke about it!' he muttered. 'I was terrfied that I might be too late. When we pulled the rock away and I saw you unconscious on the floor, my heart almost stopped.'

Standing away from the supporting column, he drew her again into the recess where the crystal nymph had kept her lonely vigil, and where the lord's son had once loved the girl from the inn. Jenna could feel their presence, and knew that Luc was sensing it too.

'I need the right to look after you,' he said deeply. 'And for that I must persuade you to marry me.' She heard a smile in his voice. 'It wouldn't be too bad, I promise! I would try to make you happy, and I think it might also please Marcel and Celestine.'

When Jenna didn't immediately answer, he cupped his hands around her rapt face. 'Could you please agree to the suggestion, my heart?'

'Yes.'

The legend had come full circle.

THE END

We do hope that you have enjoyed reading this large print book.

Did you know that all of our titles are available for purchase?

We publish a wide range of high quality large print books including:
Romances, Mysteries, Classics
General Fiction
Non Fiction and Westerns

Special interest titles available in large print are:
The Little Oxford Dictionary
Music Book, Song Book
Hymn Book, Service Book

Also available from us courtesy of Oxford University Press:
Young Readers' Dictionary
(large print edition)
Young Readers' Thesaurus
(large print edition)

For further information or a free brochure, please contact us at:
Ulverscroft Large Print Books Ltd.,
The Green, Bradgate Road, Anstey,
Leicester, LE7 7FU, England.
Tel: (00 44) **0116 236 4325**
Fax: (00 44) **0116 234 0205**

A BRIDE FOR
LORD MOUNTJOY

Karen Abbott

Georgiana's unchaperoned childhood ends when her father discovers her returning from a midnight jaunt with her brother and his friends. Squire Hailsham sends Georgiana to the Highpark Academy for Young Ladies in Brighton. There she enters High Society, where she attends elegant balls and meets dashing heroes. At the onset of a family tragedy, the eligible Lord Mountjoy crosses her path — but is he all that he seems? Does Georgiana risk breaking her heart when she discovers the truth?

VERA'S VICTORY

Anne Holman

World War II: As part of the war effort, Vera Carter has been instructed to adapt her Cordon Bleu cooking skills to running a British Restaurant in Norfolk. This is not her only worry — the staff she's been given are all untrained, and don't always get along with each other. And Geoffrey Parkington, the man in charge, seems to have very little sense of humour. But Vera soon discovers there is more to Geoffrey Parkington than she first thought . . .

FAMILY LIFE IN THE GLEN

Joan Christie

1903: Katy and Sandy Fraser's brood are fast growing up. The elder children are starting lives and families of their own, whilst the younger ones, though still at home, are starting to take their first tentative steps out into the wider world. But despite the joys it brings, family life can also be hard, and Catriona, their oldest daughter, will need everyone's support to come through tragedy and find happiness again . . .